"What I'm about to tell you is for your ears alone. Understand?"

A flicker of confusion crossed Tara's face, but she nodded.

Zach glanced around to make sure no one was listening in. "My name is Zach Davis."

She glanced at his hospital badge—Zach Reynolds—and scooted closer to her daughter.

"I'm a cop, working undercover to investigate the deaths you reported."

"You are?" she said excitedly. "Why didn't Detective Gray tell me?"

"The fewer people who know, the less likely my cover will be compromised. You are the only one at the hospital who knows why I'm really here."

"I won't tell anyone. I promise. In fact, I can help you."

"I'd appreciate that." Tara's inside knowledge could prove invaluable to closing this case quickly.

"Cop," Tara's daughter Suzie parroted. With the purple crayon clutched in her chubby fist, she drew a circle on her paper, jabbed dots in the middle and scratched two lines from the bottom. "Dak, cop," she repeated gleefully.

Zach's heart sank. This assignment had just gotten a whole lot more complicated.

Books by Sandra Orchard

Love Inspired Suspense

*Deep Cover
*Shades of Truth
*Critical Condition

*Undercover Cops

SANDRA ORCHARD

lives on a small hobby farm in rural Ontario with her real-life hero husband and college-age children. Although she taught high school math before starting her family, her childhood dream of becoming a writer never strayed far from her thoughts. She dabbled in writing articles and book reviews, but for many years needle crafts, painting and renovating a century-old farmhouse satisfied her creative appetite.

Then she discovered the world of inspirational fiction, and her writing took on new direction.

In 2009 she won the Daphne DuMaurier Award for Excellence in Mystery/Suspense, and the following year, on her "graduation day" as a home educator (i.e., her youngest daughter's first day of college), Sandra learned that Love Inspired Books wanted to publish her first novel. And so her Undercover Cops series began.

Check out her website, www.SandraOrchard.com, for interesting series extras. Sandra loves to hear from readers and can be reached through her website, on Facebook at www.Facebook.com/SandraOrchard or c/o Love Inspired Books, 233 Broadway, Suite 1001, New York, NY 10279.

CRITICAL CONDITION

SANDRA ORCHARD

Love Inspired

Recycling programs for this product may not exist in your area.

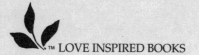

™ LOVE INSPIRED BOOKS

ISBN-13: 978-0-373-67532-6

CRITICAL CONDITION

www.LoveInspiredBooks.com

Printed in U.S.A.

The path of the righteous is like the first gleam of dawn, shining ever brighter till the full light of day.
—*Proverbs* 4:18

For Garth

THANKS:

As always to my husband and children
for their unwavering support and encouragement.
You're the best!

To my critiquers and brainstorming buddies,
Eileen Astels, Laurie Benner, Wenda Dottridge
and Vicki Talley McCollum for their encouragement
and invaluable suggestions.

To my accountability partner Patti Jo Moore
for her cyber hugs, prayers and cheers.

To my wonderful readers, blog readers and
Facebook fans who encourage and bless me in
so many ways. Your letters, posts, comments
and "likes" spur me on in the face of
uncooperative characters and plots.

And most important, thanks to my Lord Jesus
for the greatest love of all.

PROLOGUE

Strange. Tara Peterson stepped out of a patient's room only to be greeted by yet another call bell. Except this one blipped off as quickly as it sounded.

It blipped again.

A malfunction?

Seeing no sign of the other on-duty nurse, she hurried down the hall to check on the cancer patient herself. Most days she loved being a nurse. But today, she would've happily traded in her orthopedic shoes for a pair of sling-backs and a plush leather chair behind a computer monitor. Eleven and a half hours of racing from one call to another, a stack of charts awaiting her attention, made it easy to forget she hated sitting still almost as much as she hated paperwork.

She paused outside the room to ease a knot in her back and froze midstretch at the sound of something clattering across the floor, followed by a thud.

Tara threw open the door. "Mrs. Parker, what's wrong?"

The frail young woman's body stiffened, her hands

contorting at an odd angle, her unseeing eyes rolling upward.

A sudden shove propelled Tara across the room. She grabbed the bed rail, twisting her arm as momentum slammed her knees to the floor. Her head clipped the corner of the bed frame and stars exploded in front of her eyes. Biting back a cry of pain, she glanced over her shoulder in time to see the tail of a white lab coat whisk out the door.

"Wait," she shouted, a metallic taste filling her mouth.

The bed rocked frantically, but a groan snapped Tara's attention to the floor beyond, where a man lay sprawled on the cold tile. Blood spurted from a gash over his eye.

He mumbled something Tara couldn't make out.

Gritting her teeth against the white-hot pain that shot up her arm, she grabbed a towel and pressed it to his cut. "Mr. Parker, you need to hold this so I can see to your wife. Can you do that?"

Taking his grunt as a yes, Tara surged to her feet.

Mrs. Parker thrashed wildly in the throes of a seizure.

Tara pulled the code alarm, then checked Mrs. Parker's airway. Clear—for now—but the woman was burning up.

"You have to save her," Mr. Parker croaked, his tortured gaze reaching out to his wife.

Dr. Whittaker rushed into the room, his white lab coat flapping behind him.

"Give her fifty c.c.'s of diazepam stat," Whittaker barked.

Alice Bradshaw, the other nurse on duty, shoved the crash cart through the door. "I'll get it."

Dr. Whittaker steadied the patient's arm, soothing her in the dulcet tones that had earned him the moniker Dr. Wonderful from more than one patient.

As Tara tapped a vein to insert the intravenous, Mr. Parker cried out and clutched his chest.

"Take over here," Tara commanded the instant Alice returned with the diazepam. "I need to see to Mr. Parker." Pulling a stethoscope to her ears, Tara knelt at his side. Parker's breathing was shallow, his pulse thready.

Dr. McCrae hurried in and glanced from Tara to the bed, where Alice was still struggling with the IV.

"Help restrain the patient," Whittaker ordered.

Mr. Parker clutched Tara's arm and muttered a desperate prayer.

"It's okay," Tara soothed. "We're taking good care of your wife. Don't worry."

The man's gaze shifted to the team around the bed. "You have to stop—" He gasped for air. "Stop the killer."

"The killer? I don't understand. No one's been killed."

Mr. Parker's grip relaxed. And a moment later, his arm flopped lifelessly to the floor.

ONE

Detective Zach Davis turned up his collar against the brisk October weather and joined the hospital staff gathered outside Niagara's newest cancer wing. The sooner he proved a murderer wasn't behind the recent deaths at Miller's Bay Memorial, the sooner he could escape.

He couldn't imagine why a couple of deaths in a palliative-care unit—a ward where people go to die— would warrant an undercover investigation. But his former partner Rick Gray had needed a detached officer from out of town and had refused to take no for an answer.

Not that Zach had felt like explaining why this was the last place he wanted to be. He'd never told Rick he'd been married, let alone that his wife had died of cancer. As far as Rick was concerned, the five months Zach had spent posing as a computer-store owner made him the perfect candidate for his new cover as an information-technology consultant. End of discussion.

At the front of the crowd, Dr. Whittaker—the namesake of the hospital's new addition—slid giant scissor blades around the obligatory ribbon and offered the media a smile as polished as his two-hundred-dollar shoes.

As spectators jockeyed to be the first through the doors, Barb, the real IT consultant, bumped her arm against Zach's. "Come on, let's get started." The petite brunette hadn't questioned her boss's request to let Zach learn alongside her. He just hoped she'd be too distracted by her own work to notice what he really did.

He followed Barb into the happy hum of staff sharing cake and juice with patients, smiling and clothed in bathrobes and brightly colored caps. The kind of caps that masked chemo-razed hair.

His stomach knotted into a hard, tight ball.

He'd held his palm to spurting bullet wounds, wrestled drug-crazed addicts, immobilized the fractured bones of abused wives. But not one of those encounters had hit him like this, with an unnerving sense that if he looked one of these patients in the eyes, his grip on his emotions would completely unravel.

Someone—a nurse—cupped his elbow. "You okay? You've gone white."

"Yeah, I'm fine. Thanks." An antiseptic odor coiled through his nostrils, raking up memories of night-long vigils at his wife's bedside. *Lord, why have You brought me here? I don't want to remember.*

"You'd better sit a minute. You don't look so good." The nurse ushered him to a chair along the wall. "I'll bring you a glass of juice." Her compassionate voice pulled his thoughts from the edge of a dark abyss.

His colleague had kept walking, but now, her three-inch heels clicked quickly toward him. As she drew closer, her puzzled scowl softened.

Zach scraped a hand over his face. "That bad, huh?"

"Oh, yeah. I take it you don't like hospitals?"

He shook his head. "Just cancer wards."

"You lost someone close to you?"

Zach let out a heavy sigh. "Yeah." *Close.* The word didn't begin to describe what he'd lost. His wife had been everything to him. His best friend. His confidante. His very being.

The nurse hurried back with a cup of juice. "This should bring back your color. You'd be surprised how many visitors we have who get a little faint. You'll be okay in a few minutes."

He doubted more time here would do the trick, but he kept the thought to himself. Undercover work was all about attitude. With the right attitude, even in uniform, he could convince the wariest drug dealer to sell him a fix. He'd never allowed a situation to get the better of him. And he sure didn't intend to start today.

He downed the juice, crushed the cup in his hand and rose to his feet. "Thanks, I'm good to go, Miss…" Seeing the woman's doe-size brown eyes smile up at him, Zach backed into the chair's arm. A jabbing pain to his thigh anchored his feet.

"Peterson." She tilted her head as if questioning whether they'd met before. "Tara Peterson."

He blinked, then swallowed to clear the roar from his ears and the image of his dead wife standing two feet away, arm outstretched in greeting.

Not his wife. The mouth was wider, the reddish-brown hair wavier and longer. She looked a few inches taller, too. But, those eyes…

Zach blinked again, and chalked up the leap of his heart to the woman's uncanny resemblance to his wife.

Forcing a smile, he extended his hand. Then her name clicked in his brain and turned his "pleased to meet you" to paste in his mouth.

This was the nurse who'd reported the murders.

Tara glanced at the ID badge hanging from his neck, and then to Barb's. "I guess you two are the IT specialists we were warned about."

"Warned?" Zach repeated, scrambling to regain his equilibrium.

Tara chuckled. "Sure, we finally got the hang of the last system, and now you're going to change it on us again."

"I thought your present system was over five years old?" He looked to Barb for confirmation.

Barb rolled her eyes and mouthed, "Stone age."

"I heard that." Tara's grin belied her offended tone. "You computer gurus just like to torture us. But if there's anything I can do to help, don't hesitate to ask."

Zach nodded his thanks. He liked the woman's playful sense of humor. She didn't seem like the type to cry wolf. Maybe his reluctance to take the case had made his negative assessment of its merits too hasty.

Zach shadowed Barb for most of the day to acquaint himself with the job. Then he forced himself to return to the cancer ward, where the alleged murders had occurred. Implementing a new software system gave him a perfect excuse to question staff, not to mention peek at their online activities.

As he passed the staff lounge, a commotion erupted.

"You have to let this go," a female voice soothed.

"I won't let it go. Someone murdered those people." Zach recognized Tara's voice and the flint of pain behind her words.

"The coroner disagrees," the other woman responded.

"For all we know the murderer paid him off."

Zach tensed. The last thing he needed were rumors of a killing spree spreading through the hospital.

"You're talking crazy," a different woman spoke up.

"Am I? Someone shoved me into the bed. Clearly, he didn't want to be seen."

"Are you sure you didn't just trip? You hit your head pretty hard."

"No!" The slap of a hand against a table punctuated the denial. "How many times do I have to tell you? Someone murdered Mrs. Parker. Her husband begged me to stop the killer."

Zach rushed to the door. Tara might as well have painted a bull's-eye on her forehead. He needed to get her out of there before she made the situation any worse.

Two nurses and a doctor were in the room with her. Tara reached for a lunch container in the fridge and deposited it into a cloth bag on her arm. Absorbed in the discussion, no one acknowledged his arrival.

"I was there and I didn't hear Mr. Parker say anything," the older nurse said. "How about you, Dr. McCrae?"

The young resident standing at the counter with his coffee shook his head. "Afraid not." He took a sip from his mug and shot Tara a sympathetic look.

"Well, I know what I heard." Tara's voice sharpened. "And if the police won't—"

"Miss Peterson…" Zach tapped on the door. "Sorry to interrupt, but I need your help."

Looking a little stunned, Tara lifted her gaze to his. "My help?"

"With the computer setup for your nurse's station." When she hesitated, it was all he could do not to grab her by the wrist and yank her out of the room. Something he should've done the instant he'd heard the word *murderer* come out of her mouth. "Please."

"Yes, of course." She followed him to the door, and he motioned her to go ahead of him.

Dr. Whittaker passed them with a cursory glance. "What was all that yelling about?" he asked, stepping into the staff lounge.

"Tara was ranting about the murderer again," one of the nurses said.

Zach couldn't make out Whittaker's riled response—something about bad press—but Tara must've heard, because she clenched her fingers into a fist.

"I can't believe the police aren't doing anything," she muttered.

Zach steered her to the privacy of the empty nurse's station. "About what?" he asked, since she had no idea why he was really here. He couldn't believe that she'd all but thrown down the gauntlet for a murderer to come after her.

Maybe he should have taken Rick up on the option to let her in on the operation.

Clearly heartened by his interest, Tara seemed to forget about his computer questions and explained in detail what happened the night of Mr. and Mrs. Parker's alleged murders.

He nodded as if it were all news to him. "I can see how important finding this person is to you, but you might not want to broadcast your intentions."

Her face blanched. "You think he'd come after me?"

"It sounds like you're the only witness."

"But I didn't see who shoved me," she insisted.

"He—or she—wouldn't know that. Chances are that he didn't even know whom he'd shoved out of his way until…"

Tara's bottom lip trembled. "Until I opened my mouth."

Offering an empathetic smile, Zach nudged her toward a desk chair. "You weren't exactly keeping your voice down."

Her teeth dug into her lip, stilling the tremble, and the vulnerability in her eyes—those enormous eyes he couldn't tear his gaze from—completely undid him.

She sank into the chair. "What am I going to do?"

"I'd suggest stop talking about what you saw."

"I can't. You don't understand…. There have been other suspicious deaths."

The anguish in her voice had him debating whether he'd be better off letting her in on his undercover operation. If she kept up these tirades, she'd not only give the supposed murderer a reason to silence her, she'd make Zach's job a whole lot tougher. "Suspicious how?" he asked, pulling a chair next to hers. He scrolled through a couple of computer screens so they'd appear to be looking over the new software.

"Sudden, inexplicable fevers. Besides Mr. and Mrs. Parker's death last week, we had an incident a couple of months ago, and another, Ellen Clark, the night before last. But the police still won't believe me. If only I'd done more to convince them…" Her voice hitched. "I might have saved her."

Rick had told Zach about Miss Clark. The woman had been presented in the E.R. with the same symptoms as Debra Parker.

"The doctors and nurse who tried to resuscitate Mrs. Parker say I'm crazy." Tara's fingers did a frenetic dance along the edge of the table, and Zach had to resist the urge to still them. "They say the high fever triggered the seizure that killed Debra. But they can't explain the fever."

"How do your colleagues account for the husband's death?"

"Dr. Whittaker figures that witnessing his wife's

seizure triggered a heart attack and made Mr. Parker spout the—" Tara made air quotes "—*nonsense* about stopping a killer. But someone else was in that hospital room." She held up her bandaged wrist. "That's how I got this. And he's already struck again. Don't you see? That's why I can't stay quiet."

That's what Zach was afraid of. Maybe the smartest thing would be to tell her he was a cop.

"Do you realize you're the first person who's taken my concerns seriously?"

Zach lowered his voice. "I'm sorry you've been made to feel that way. And I am concerned, especially if this person has figured out you're a witness." He recognized the moment his implication sank in.

Tara's determined expression wilted, but then she suddenly bolted to her feet. "My daughter."

Zach's heart skidded to a halt at the thought of a killer going after her child. "Where is she?"

"The hospital daycare. You don't think—?" Tara raced to the elevator without finishing the thought he could guess all too well.

He rushed after her.

The elevator doors closed before Tara reached them. She slapped the button, and when they didn't reopen, she took off down the stairwell.

"Tara, wait," Zach called after her. He'd wanted to scare some sense into her, not scare her senseless. He had to tell her who he really was.

At the bottom of the stairs, he caught her arm and

hauled her to a stop. "You need to calm down." He gripped her shoulders. "You don't want your little girl to sense your fear, do you?"

The air swooshed from her lungs. "No, but—"

"Shh." He touched his fingertips to her lips, and a jab of awareness pinged through him. What was he doing?

Her eyes grew even larger, if that were possible.

Instantly, he dropped his hands to his sides. He wanted to tell her she wasn't in any danger, but after hearing her account firsthand, he wasn't so sure anymore. "I need to tell you something."

A door above them banged open.

Instinctively, Zach stepped between Tara and the stairs. A couple of housekeepers hurried down a flight and exited on the next floor. "Let's talk outside," Zach suggested.

"Not until I get Suzie." Tara's voice edged higher.

Zach cringed. This wasn't a conversation he wanted to have in front of her daughter. "She'll be safe in the daycare."

Tara glanced at her watch. "My shift finished ten minutes ago—she'll be expecting me." Tara yanked open the stairwell door and strode to the daycare center.

Zach waited in the hallway, debating whether he should call Rick before disclosing his true occupation. But one glimpse of the rosy-cheeked tot Tara swept into her arms had him deciding he'd rather remind

Rick, after the fact, that he'd given Zach that option. When Tara emerged carrying the girl on one hip, Zach gave the child a goofy grin. "Hey, Suzie, my name's Zach. How old are you?"

The tot smushed her baby finger and thumb against her palm and proudly displayed three fingers.

"Three, wow! You're a big girl."

Her golden ringlets bobbed as she stretched herself taller, straining the seams of her yellow jumper.

"Careful, honey," Tara singsonged in that sweet, high-pitched tone women seemed to use with anyone under two and a half feet. "Mommy's wrist is sore. Remember?"

Suzie thrust her arms into the air and flung herself toward Zach.

Swallowing his surprise, he scooped her into his arms. "I got you, you little munchkin. We're giving Mommy's boo-boo a rest, are we?"

"I'm sorry." Tara reached for the child.

"That's okay. I don't mind carrying her for you."

A strange expression flitted across Tara's face, followed by a manufactured smile. Her arms dropped to her sides. "Thank you."

Considering her contradictory response, he didn't know whether to apologize or say "you're welcome." So he led the way to the back exit. A mirror hung by the door. Zach tapped Suzie's reflection. "Who's that?"

She splayed her palm on her chest and gave herself a huge smile. "Me!"

"You," Zach agreed with a chuckle, mesmerized by the chocolate gaze so like her mother's.

Suzie lunged for the glass, almost toppling out of his arms. He caught her just as her chubby fingers smacked against his startled reflection. "Dak!"

His heart suddenly felt too big for his chest. "That's right. My name's Zach." He glanced at Tara's reflection, but she seemed intent on avoiding his gaze. He half expected her to make an excuse, take back her daughter and leave.

But she opened the door and led the way to a picnic table at the edge of the daycare's playground. Clearly, she was desperate for a compatriot to her cause. She dug a notepad and crayons from her oversized handbag and then patted the seat beside her. "Come and draw, honey, while the grown-ups talk."

Suzie bounced in Zach's arms, apparently a three-year-old's signal for *put me down*.

He swooped her onto the seat, airplane-style, and earned himself another giant smile.

"You're very good with children." Tara's timid smile came slower than her daughter's. "Suzie usually doesn't take to men."

Zach shrugged off the compliment and snagged the seat opposite them.

Now that Tara had her daughter at her side, the panic in her eyes had waned. Of course, if it waned too much, she might shoot off her mouth again, and he couldn't afford to take that risk. A killer wasn't likely to let her live if he figured she could identify him. "What I'm about to tell you is for your ears alone. Understand?"

A flicker of confusion crossed her face, but she nodded.

"You can't discuss it with your colleagues, your friends, not even your husband." Oh, man, what was he thinking?

"My ex-husband walked out on us a long time ago." She ducked her head, as if embarrassed at admitting something so personal to a practical stranger. Oddly, she didn't feel like a stranger to him.

"I'm sorry." Zach looked at Suzie, his heart cracking at the thought of the fun daddy things she was missing out on in her young life. He stopped himself before considering what Tara was missing, too.

She was a witness. A contact. Nothing more.

Exhaling sharply, he glanced around to make sure no one was listening in. "My name is Zach Davis."

Her gaze dropped to the name on his hospital badge—Zach Reynolds—and she scooted closer to her daughter.

"I'm a cop, working undercover to investigate the deaths you reported."

Her face lit up. "You are? Why didn't Detective Gray tell me?"

"The fewer people who know, the less likely my cover will be compromised." He leaned across the table and lowered his voice. "You are the only one at the hospital who knows why I'm really here, and we need to keep it that way."

"I won't tell anyone.... I promise. In fact, I can help you."

"I'd appreciate that." Zach breathed his first full breath since considering whether to tell her. Tara's inside knowledge could prove invaluable to closing this case quickly.

"Cop," Suzie parroted. With the purple crayon clutched in her chubby fist, she drew a circle on her paper, jabbed dots in the middle and scratched two lines from the bottom. "Dak, cop," she repeated gleefully.

Zach's heart sank. He sent a prayer heavenward. This assignment had just gotten a whole lot more complicated.

No, this couldn't be happening. If they were going to stop the killer from striking again, she had to make her daughter understand. Tara cupped Suzie's face between her hands. "Look at me, sweetie. Zach's a computer consultant. *Not* a cop. Okay?"

"Not a cop."

"That's right. So you mustn't say he is."

"Not a cop," Suzie repeated.

Zach looked even paler than he had after Suzie drew his picture.

Tara turned over the paper. "Don't worry," she said, with more confidence than she felt. "Suzie won't blow your cover."

Zach didn't look so sure. "Maybe you could take some time off until I've finished the investigation. After your outburst in the lounge, we'd probably be safer all around."

She thought of how panicked she'd felt only a few minutes ago. Now that she knew the police were on the case, she didn't feel nearly so worried. She hadn't said anything in that room that her colleagues hadn't already heard. And sure, she might've momentarily suspected McCrae and Whittaker the night of the murder when they'd run into the room wearing the same kind of lab coats as the guy who'd shoved her, but if one of them was worried about her identifying them, he would've done something by now. "It's okay. I'll keep my mouth shut and my eyes open. I'm a single mom with bills to pay. I can't afford to take time off."

"I understand. But you must have vacation time available. Or, given your wrist injury, we could probably arrange a paid medical leave."

"Absolutely not. My promotion to head nurse last month earned me flack from more than one nurse with seniority over me. I will not give them the ammunition to take me out."

A muscle in Zach's jaw twitched. "It's okay," he said in a comforting tone that sounded as though he meant it. He tousled Suzie's hair. "Once this little munchkin sees me around the hospital, she'll probably start calling me Doc."

Suzie patted his arm. "Dak."

Zach winked at Tara. "What did I tell you?"

Her stomach did a tiny flip. Zach didn't act the way she'd expect a detective to act at all. With his bronzed skin and sandy-blond hair, he looked as though he spent more time on a surfboard than at a computer. She didn't want to try to decipher the twinge of admiration she'd felt when Suzie had taken so readily to him. Her little girl wouldn't even go to Grandma as willingly as she'd belly flopped into Zach's strong arms.

Tara shook her head. How would she know if his arms were strong?

It's not that Suzie weighed very much. Any guy's muscles would bulge when he flexed his arms to lift a child. *Oh, brother, get off what his arms look like already.* She cleared her throat. "Um, do you really think the…" Glancing at her daughter, she mouthed the word *killer.* "…would come after me?"

"What can you tell me about the patients who died?"

Tara blinked. Assuming his answer might hinge on hers, she said, "They were all Dr. Whittaker's patients. Different ages. Different types of cancer. Unlike Ellen, the first two patients were already on the ward when their fevers struck."

"Wealthy?"

"Not that I know of. Why?"

"We need a motive," he explained. "Why do you think someone would murder these people?"

"I don't know. I never thought about it, except in Mr. Parker's case. I assumed he surprised the killer."

"You told Detective Gray this person wore a lab coat."

"Yes."

"Did you notice a scent? Any sound? The squeak of shoes, maybe? The color of his pants?"

Tara closed her eyes and tried to remember. "Yes!" Her eyes popped open. "His pants were dark blue. But…" She inhaled, focused her mind on the memories of that night. But all she could smell was Zach's woodsy scent. Her heart fluttered. She shook her head. "I'm sorry, I can't recall anything else."

"If you do, let me know. In the meantime, I'll look for evidence of fudged medical reports, manipulated drug trials or threatened lawsuits—anything that points to a possible motive. I need you to alert me to any unusual behavior on the part of staff or patients. Okay?"

"Absolutely. But…" She dug her fingers into her palms. "Um… You didn't answer my question. Do you think he'll come after me?"

"Do you have a cell phone?"

"Yes." She looked at him quizzically, then pulled it from her purse.

He took it and punched in numbers. "I've programmed in my number. If you notice anything unusual or suspicious, if anything frightens you, don't hesitate to call me. Day or night. Understand?"

Her pulse raced. "Yes, but you didn't answer my question."

"Do you live alone?"

"Yes." Fear welled in her throat. He *did* think she'd be a target. He must.

"Is there somewhere else you can stay for a while? A friend's perhaps?"

"Are you trying to scare me?" she said through gritted teeth, not wanting to believe what his avoidance was saying loud and clear. "Is this another tactic to get me to take time off work?"

"No."

"Then answer my question."

Zach's gaze shifted to Suzie and his voice dropped to a whisper. "Yes, Tara, I believe you could be in danger."

TWO

The next day, with half a night of prayer behind him, Zach managed to walk the halls of the cancer ward without feeling that he might faint. Good thing, too, since the realization that Tara's theories might not be so far-fetched had nixed all hope of avoiding this area of the hospital.

Barbara's finely plucked eyebrows had disappeared into her bangs when he'd offered to test the computer setups in the new wing. But once he'd convinced his colleague that he would rather confront his ghosts than run from them, she had handed over the pass cards to all the computers on the floor.

Ahead of him, Tara stepped from a patient's room. Her hair was done up in a funky bun. Strands of hair poked out in various directions, and several wayward tendrils curled down the back of her slender neck. Oh, boy, if his mouth went this dry watching her from behind, he dreaded to think how he'd react to seeing those beautiful brown eyes again.

She turned, and her smile swept the breath from his lungs.

He recovered quickly and asked for directions to Whittaker's office. He knew the way, but asking Tara to show him would give him an opportunity to find out how she was faring without piquing anyone's curiosity.

Tara glanced at the pass cards he held. "Dr. Whittaker doesn't like to be disturbed too soon after rounds. Perhaps you could start with our resident's computer. Dr. McCrae."

Recognizing the name as one of the doctors on duty the night the Parkers died, Zach agreed.

"How are you doing?" he asked as they strolled to McCrae's office.

"I didn't sleep so well. I thought I'd sleep better, knowing you're…you know. But I woke at every noise, worried he'd come after me."

"I'm sorry I scared you. But I'd rather you be on your guard than unaware of potential danger. Suzie okay?"

Tara chuckled. "Oh, yeah. You made quite an impression on her. All evening it was Dak this, and Dak that."

Zach smiled past a pang of grief. "She's a sweet girl."

Tara knocked on an unmarked door. When there was no response, she pushed it open. "Before this new wing was added, our interns and residents got nothing more than a locker and had to share computers with the nurses. But Dr. Whittaker insisted that, since residents work such long shifts, they should be given an office." She chuckled and jutted her chin toward the far corner. "The mattress was McCrae's idea."

Zach surveyed the small room, doing his best not to inhale Tara's vanilla scent as she moved toward the window. With the bare white walls, chrome-and-glass desk and slatted window blinds, the office looked as sterile as an examination room. He supposed residents weren't around long enough to add those personal touches that would offer some hint of their life outside the hospital.

Zach settled into a plush leather desk chair, pausing to appreciate the improvement over the cheap box-store chair he'd had on his last case. "Any news on Miss Clark's cause of death?" he asked, now that they wouldn't be overheard.

"Not yet." She frowned and twisted open the vertical blinds. The light striped her face like prison bars. "For all we know, the coroner could be in cahoots with whomever's behind this."

The anger fueling her comment didn't mask the wobble in her voice. An aching vulnerability that awakened every protective instinct in him. Taking a moment to reel in his emotions, he powered up the computer. "I'll check him out. You said the patient asked for you before she died. Anyone inquire about that?"

"Actually, Dr. Whittaker commended me for having such a positive impact on our patients that they'd ask for me by name. Not that his comment surprised me. He's always upbeat and encouraging."

"Hmm, a regular Dr. Wonderful," Zach said, repeating the moniker he'd overheard one of the nurses use for the man.

Tara shrugged. "He's nice."

As Zach waited for the computer to boot, he motioned Tara to shut the door and peeked inside McCrae's desk.

Suddenly, he heard loud footsteps in the hallway. The door banged off the wall, and a doctor stormed in, lab coat flapping in his wake, his face as red as his hair. "What are you doing in my office?"

"This is Zach Reynolds," Tara answered for him. "He's the IT specialist who's upgrading our computer systems. I showed him in."

McCrae's gaze flashed to Zach and then down to where his hand hovered over an open drawer.

Zach snagged a pen from inside. "You don't mind if I borrow this, do you? Mine's run out." Without waiting for a response, Zach slid the security pass card into the new hub that would connect McCrae's monitor to the main network. "I could be a couple of hours getting this set up. Were you needing access before I start?"

McCrae plunged his balled hands into the pockets of his lab coat. "No, that's fine. I have patients to see." He strode past Tara and scooped his stethoscope off the desktop. "Next time, however, I'd appreciate being informed before you barge into my office." McCrae gave the room a sweeping glance and then left as quickly as he'd appeared.

"Whew, quick temper on that one." Zach tossed the borrowed pen back into the drawer.

"It's the sleep deprivation. Makes the residents edgy. He's quite tenderhearted once you get to know him."

"How will I ever come up with possible suspects if you have such high opinions of everyone on staff?"

Tara snorted. "Wait until you meet Alice Bradshaw."

"Who's she?"

"A nurse who... Well, let's just say that when it comes to Alice, I follow my dear departed grandma's advice. 'If you can't say something nice about a person, don't say—'"

Zach flashed Tara a silencing glance as a gray-haired nurse stepped into the doorway.

Tara spun toward the door. At the sight of her least favorite person in the world, she swallowed the last of her words. Okay, maybe Alice Bradshaw wasn't her least favorite person.

Her rat-fink ex-husband, who'd split on her and their then eight-week-old daughter, held that distinction.

But what was Alice doing here? Spying on her?

It was high time the woman figured out that twenty years' seniority didn't give her license to mind everyone else's business. Tara took a deep breath.

Okay, Alice had caught Tara talking about her. Not good. But if she let on that she was the least bit rattled, Alice would pounce. Ever since Tara's promotion, Alice had snatched every possible opportunity to undermine her authority.

Zach's gaze ping-ponged from Alice to her, and the twinkle in his eye tugged a smile to her lips. She turned the smile to Alice. "Was there something you needed?"

Alice blinked, clearly surprised that her ability to unnerve Tara had lost its effect, but she recovered quickly. "Yes, actually." Her ultraprim voice enunciated each syllable with precision. "The patients are waiting for their meds."

Tara glanced at her watch and inwardly cringed at how late it was. "Okay, thank you. I'll be right there."

When Tara returned her attention to Zach, a dimple dented his cheek. "I see what you mean," he said. Then, all hint of humor faded as he added, "Stay alert. We'll talk later."

The rest of the morning passed in a blur. Every bed on the ward was full, and every other patient had some urgent crisis demanding her attention. She was grateful for the distraction, but still found herself struggling to focus on her work, because busy as she was, she couldn't shake the uneasy feeling that had her looking over her shoulder every few minutes.

She was three bites into her lunch when the front office paged her. On her way there, she passed through the lobby, where Dr. Whittaker was showing a group of well-heeled prospects the inscribed marble donor wall on which their generosity would be forever immortalized.

Tara had to chuckle. He went on and on about the groundbreaking research they'd be supporting, but everyone knew it was his irresistible charisma that pulled in the donations.

A newly inscribed block at the end of the wall caught Tara's attention, and she skidded to a stop. *Mr. and Mrs. Parker, platinum donors?*

They hadn't had that kind of money. Mr. Parker had often lamented about the extra jobs he had to take to afford his wife's natural supplements, and how he hated that work kept him from being with her more.

A hand clamped her upper arm, jolting her from her thoughts.

"Miss Peterson?" Dr. Whittaker smiled down at her with his perfect white teeth. "For a moment, you looked like you might faint."

His gaze strayed to the Parker inscription, his forehead creasing.

Zach's words—stay alert—pulsed in her ears as Whittaker shifted, blocking her from the view of the potential donors he was courting. "No, I'm fine. I…" She peeked around him at their audience and raised her voice for their benefit. "I was admiring how generous people have been."

Dr. Whittaker beamed and shifted again, no doubt hoping her accolades would inspire further generosity.

She tapped her finger on the Parkers' name to gauge his reaction. "This couple, for example. They must've bequeathed their entire estate to this project."

"Yes, the late Mr. and Mrs. Parker were extremely charitable." His lips jitterbugged from a smile to a frown before finally settling into a grim line. Although obviously pleased by the coup, he knew enough not to show his pleasure, considering the couple had to *die* for the hospital to get the money.

Tara stiffened. *Motive.*

He certainly had means and opportunity. Who would ever suspect Dr. Wonderful of being the grim reaper?

Tara's gaze shot to his. He still held her by the arm. And his grip was tightening.

Zach strode toward them like a gleaming knight. He tapped the doctor's shoulder. "Excuse me, Dr. Whittaker?"

Whittaker's grip loosened. "Yes?"

Zach thrust out his hand, leaving Whittaker no choice but to release her and extend his own hand.

Tara mouthed a thank-you and then scurried away without a backward glance. What was she thinking, goading Whittaker like that?

That's the trouble—she didn't think. Mom always warned her she was too impulsive. Had Whittaker read her suspicions in her expression? Or was he just trying to stop her babbling before someone made the connection between the names on the wall and the recent deaths?

Either way, if *Dr. Wonderful* sensed she didn't buy into the persona he was peddling, she was in trouble.

Her stomach roiled at the thought. She dealt quickly with the front office's questions, and then returned to the lunchroom. But she was so rattled that her stomach grew queasier by the second. She covered the macaroni salad she'd barely touched and returned the container to the staff fridge.

She tried to focus on paperwork to take her mind off her suspicions of Whittaker. Surely Zach would come by to ask about the run-in. She'd never had such a bad case of nerves. The detective's warnings must've spooked her more than she'd realized. The mix of concern and determination she'd seen in his eyes as he'd drawn up behind Whittaker flittered through her thoughts. That…and how Zach's shirt had strained across his broad chest when he'd reached up and tapped Whittaker's shoulder.

Maybe suspicions weren't the only things leaving her a little rattled.

Unable to attend to the paperwork, Tara waited for Alice to go on her break. Then she slipped into the back room where the medicines were kept. For days she'd been meaning to inventory the medicine locker to see if she could figure out what drug might've been used to kill the Parkers. Trouble was, Mr. and Mrs. Parker's divergent symptoms suggested two different drugs, and none of the standard culprits had shown up in the coroner's tox screen. Motive alone wouldn't be enough reason for Zach to arrest Whittaker. They had to figure out how he did it. If, in fact, he *had* done it.

"Peterson."

Tara jumped at Whittaker's gruff summons and fumbled the bottle of oxycodone she was holding.

He snagged the bottle before it hit the floor,

squinted at the label, then at her. "Your wrist still bothering you?"

"No," she huffed, appalled by the insinuation that she'd sneak a pain pill. She hadn't even filled the Tylenol 3 prescription the E.R. doc had given her the night of the incident. "I'm inventorying the medicine locker."

His foot kicked the doorstop. The door closed with a thud.

Suddenly the room felt far too small, and she wished Alice were still here.

"Alice tells me you were late dispensing meds this morning."

Scratch Alice. Tara wished Zach were here. She backed up a step only to have the handle of a spare bedside table press into her back. "Yes, sir."

Whittaker raised an eyebrow. "No excuse?"

"It wouldn't change the fact."

"Hmm." His stern expression relaxed. "Yes, some things are better kept to ourselves." He rolled the narcotics bottle between his fingers. "Wouldn't you agree?"

"Um, I suppose."

"Good." He plopped the bottle back on the shelf. "I'm glad we understand each other."

"Excuse me?" Her voice pitched higher. But the instant the question escaped her lips, she bit her tongue. Would she never learn?

He'd probably been seconds away from walking out of the room and now…he was standing there gritting his teeth. The table handle dug deeper into her back.

"The Parkers' deaths were an unfortunate occurrence that Memorial happened to benefit from." Whittaker's slow, measured words sucked the air from her lungs, one agonizing molecule at a time. "The less attention drawn to that fact, the better. We wouldn't want people to get the wrong ideas. Would *we?*" He yanked open the door and stalked out.

This time Tara couldn't ignore her upset stomach. She grabbed a bedpan and heaved.

Alice's head poked in the door. "I thought I heard someone in here. Oh, you don't look so good." She helped Tara to a chair in the nurses' station. "What is it? The flu?"

"I don't know. It—" Cramps seized Tara's stomach. She doubled over, moaning.

"I'll get you something to calm the nausea." Alice exchanged the bedpan with a clean one and rushed off. A few minutes later, she returned with a syringe. "Dr. Whittaker said I could give you an injection so it'll work faster."

"No, I don't think—" Another wave hit, and this time Tara ran for the sink.

"Trust me. It'll help." Alice swabbed Tara's arm and administered the injection before Tara could object again. "Now, why don't you lie down in the locker room to give the medicine time to work? I'll cover for you."

The panic Zach had seen in Tara's eyes had gripped his emotions and wouldn't let go. He yanked the pass card from the computer hub he'd been testing and headed for the nurses' station. After witnessing the hold Whittaker had had on Tara's arm, he'd thought the hospital's Golden Boy might be their man, but after talking with him, Zach wasn't so sure. He needed to hear Tara's version of what had gone down in the lobby at lunchtime.

The nurses' station was vacant. He walked up and down the halls, glancing in patients' rooms, but found no sign of her. Anxiety mounting, he checked the staff lounge.

Alice Bradshaw glanced up. "Looking for someone?" she asked in that gratingly precise tone of hers.

"Yes, the head nurse."

"That would be me."

Alarm bells went off in Zach's head. "You? I thought Miss Peterson—"

"She went home sick. I'm covering for her. Can I help you with something?"

"It can wait. Thanks." He went back to the computer he'd been testing, but a niggling uneasiness made concentrating impossible. Only yesterday, Tara had outright refused to take time off. He pulled out his cell phone and dialed her number.

After five rings, voice mail kicked in.

He clicked End without leaving a message. If she felt sick, she'd probably gone straight to bed. He wandered past Whittaker's office, and at the sight of him frowning at the computer monitor, breathed a relieved sigh.

Zach shook his head. What was he thinking? That

Whittaker would hunt her down with some threatening reprimand?

If she felt scared, she would've come to him. Even so, the acid burning his stomach showed no sign of abating. He borrowed the phone book from the nurses' station to look up her address. But there were three columns of Petersons, and not one had a first initial *T.* He called Rick.

"What's up?"

"I need Tara's address. Something weird went down at lunchtime, and she left early. I need to make sure she's okay."

Rick rattled off the address. "Do you think she's in danger?"

"I wouldn't be asking for the address otherwise, would I?" Zach snapped. "I'll be in touch."

He clamped down his riled emotions and hurried out to the hospital parking lot. *Lord, please let me be overreacting.*

Consulting the map he'd picked up in the hospital gift shop, he wound through three unmarked subdivisions before finding Pine Street. He pinpointed Tara's house and slowed to a crawl. The driveway was empty.

He double-checked the house number against the one Rick had given him. *Same.* His pulse spiked. All afternoon, concern had nagged him. Clearly, he should've paid more attention.

He tried her cell phone again.

"Hello?"

Zach's heart leaped at the sound of her voice. "Tara, where are you? Bradshaw said you were sick."

"Yeah, I am. I brought Suzie to my mom's for the night."

"You're at your mom's?"

"Just leavin—"

Tara screamed and what sounded like gunfire blasted over the phone.

"Tara? Tara? Talk to me. Tell me where you are."

THREE

Screams—her own screams—barraged Tara's eardrums. She dove face-first into the front seat of the car and covered her head with her arms.

The window behind her seat shattered, spraying glass over the seats, her clothes, her hair.

"Tara, talk to me!" Zach's voice shrilled from the vicinity of the floorboard.

She took one hand from her head and felt for her cell phone. If she hadn't been reaching into the car to grab the phone, that first shot might've gone through her heart instead of through her car and out the passenger window.

Her fingers closed around the phone as another shot ripped through the door. Clinging to the phone, she rolled to the floor. Pebbles of glass ground into her legs and arms. "Someone's shooting at me!"

"Are you okay?"

"Someone's shooting at me!"

"Where are you?" he demanded.

"In my car."

"I need an address!"

The sound of screeching tires pierced the air. "I think he's gone. I hear sirens coming. I'll just—"

"Tara, stay down." The urgency in Zach's voice knocked her back with all the force of a physical push. "Don't lift your head. Tell me where you are."

"Sam's Cove. Thirty-eight Eagle Avenue. It's ten minutes west of Miller's Bay."

"I'm on my way, but stay on the line. Are the sirens getting closer?"

The steady timbre of his voice eased her heart's frantic pounding. "Yes."

"Good. Someone must've called it in. Stay down until the cops get there."

She swiped at a tear dripping down her cheek and gasped when her hand came away bloody.

"What's wrong?"

"I'm bleeding."

"Were you hit?"

"It's just from the shattered glass, I think. I don't know...." She felt herself losing control. "Zach, I can't stay here. What if the shooter comes closer?" Except she couldn't run for the house and draw gunfire near Suzie.

"Stay calm. Put pressure on the wound. I'll be there as fast as I can. Just hold on."

At the sound of feet pounding toward her, she curled deeper into the narrow space beneath the dash.

A hulking figure appeared at the door, blocking the light.

Tara couldn't help it. She screamed.

"What is it?" Zach asked urgently.

"Tara, it's me."

Relief poured through her as she recognized the voice of her mom's neighbor John Calloway.

The older gentleman gingerly pulled her free of the glass. "Let me get you inside." He tried to pry the phone from her clenched fist. "The police are on their way. Your daughter is screaming for you, and it's all your mom can do to hold her."

Suzie's cry fired Tara's muscles. She dropped the phone and ran to the front door, where Mom held her thrashing daughter by the waist. The instant her mother released the child, Suzie tumbled into Tara's arms.

Mr. Calloway herded them inside the house.

Within seconds, an explosion of colored lights strobed through the window, dancing across the walls of the tiny living room.

Tara collapsed into an armchair, and Suzie burrowed into her arms, sobbing. "It's okay, baby. Mommy's okay."

Tara's mom shook her head, but thankfully didn't voice her disagreement.

"Did you see the shooter?" Mr. Calloway asked.

"No."

"You must have seen something," Mom pressed, her voice edging higher.

Tara squeezed Suzie more tightly and gave her mother a *not now* look.

Mr. Calloway shook his head. "You never saw

things like this when I was a kid. It's the drugs. Seems to be all kids care about these days. The cops say they broke up that local drug ring, but I don't believe it. Before long we'll be no different than those American cities you see on TV."

Her mother slipped from the room and reappeared with a damp facecloth. She gently dabbed at Tara's face. "The cut doesn't look too bad. I don't think you'll need stitches." The cloth came away bloody, and Mom's wary expression belied the calm in her voice.

Through the window, Tara could see an officer unfurling caution tape as another pointed in the direction from which the shots had likely been fired. She shivered. Drive-by shootings weren't supposed to happen in quiet communities where churches outnumbered bars four to one.

A loud rap sounded at the door. Mr. Calloway let in a uniformed police officer and directed him to Tara.

The officer removed his hat. "I'm Officer Nelson, ma'am. I need to ask you some questions." His gaze shifted from her to Suzie.

Mom reached for Suzie's hand. "Come on, sweetheart. Grandma will get you some milk and cookies while your mommy talks to the police officer."

"No." Suzie's arms clamped around Tara's middle. "I not leave you."

"It's okay, sweetie." Tara lifted her daughter's chin. "We're all safe inside the house with the officer here to protect us. I need you to be a big, brave girl. Okay?"

Mom gently cupped Suzie's shoulders and tugged

her away. Mr. Calloway hovered at the door, looking uncertain whether to stay or go.

The officer pulled out a pad and pen. "Did you see who shot at you?"

She wedged her trembling hands under her legs. "No."

"Has anyone threatened you? A jilted boyfriend maybe?"

"No!" she retorted.

"You having any domestic problems? A business deal go bad?"

Momentarily speechless at the suggestion that she brought the attack on herself, Tara crossed her arms. "No."

"It's got to be drugs," Mr. Calloway muttered. "It's always about drugs."

"I'll take your statement in a few minutes, sir. If you wouldn't mind waiting in the kitchen, I'd appreciate it."

Mr. Calloway let out a snort, but did as he was asked.

Officer Nelson flipped over a page of his notepad. "Okay, then tell me everything you can remember—descriptions of any people or cars you saw pass by before the shooting."

"I didn't notice anyone. I left work sick." Thankfully, she didn't feel too sick anymore. The overload of adrenaline coursing through her system must've flushed out whatever had been cramping her stomach. That and the shot Alice had given her. "I brought my daughter here to my mom's so I could go home and sleep."

The sound of squealing brakes snapped her attention

to the living-room window. A black pickup screeched to a stop at the end of the driveway, nose-to-nose with a cruiser. Zach jumped out.

Her heart kicked at the sight of him plowing past the police tape, a mix of determination and worry creasing his handsome face.

A burly cop yanked him back.

"That's my friend," Tara told Officer Nelson. "Can you ask your officers to let him through?"

Nelson opened the front door. "It's okay, Joe. Give him clearance."

Zach didn't wait. He sprinted through the door and to her side. His eyes roamed her entire body, settling on the cut above her left brow. A mixture of anger and relief churned in his eyes. "Are you okay?"

She nodded, her mouth suddenly too dry to speak, given the turbulent emotions parading across his face. He was a cop. Yet he looked as though his insides had gone through a meat grinder, the utter opposite of Nelson's detached expression.

The officer bombarded her with a dozen more questions, then took Mr. Calloway outside for his version.

Suzie flew around the corner with Mom on her heels.

Zach scooped Suzie into the air. "Whoa there, kiddo." He planted her back on her feet, and Suzie's face lit into the first smile Tara had seen since they'd arrived.

Suzie curled her shoulders forward, scrunching her arms against her chest, looking shy. "Hi, Dak."

"Hey there, Suzie." He scooped a dollop of chocolate from her cheek. "Mmm, what have you been eating?"

"Cupcakes."

"Could I have one?"

She gave him a big nod, and then looked to Tara.

"You can bring us each one, sweetie." As Suzie raced back into the kitchen on her new mission, Tara said to her mom, "We need a few more minutes. If you can manage it…"

"Who is—?"

"Mom, please. I'll explain later."

Mom gave Zach a curious look, but headed back to the kitchen. Tara could always count on her to put Suzie's welfare first.

"Who knew you were coming here?" Zach asked the moment her mother disappeared.

"No one. I only decided to come as I was leaving the hospital parking lot."

"Did you notice anyone following you?"

"No." Her breath caught, her thoughts racing. "You don't think this has something to do with the deaths at the hospital, do you?"

"We need to consider the possibility."

"The officer said they had a drive-by shooting just last month. That this was probably a case of mistaken identity. They know an ex-gang member lives in a house like this a few blocks over."

Zach hunkered down in front of her and lowered his voice to an earnest whisper. "Officer Nelson is likely right, but I'd rather err on the side of caution. Is there somewhere else you could stay for a while? At least until we figure out who's responsible?"

The churning in her stomach returned. Why was this happening to her? Life was hard enough, juggling a job and Suzie's care. She couldn't bear to be driven from her home, too. "No one followed me here," she insisted. "I want to go home. Suzie is frightened enough. If I take her somewhere else, she'll only become more scared."

Zach's gaze was filled with compassion, but she could see the mental debate going on behind his eyes.

"Even if your concerns were founded," she said, "I can't bring danger to someone else's doorstep. My phone number is unlisted." Tara waved her hand toward the window. "My car obviously won't be in the driveway. Suzie and I will be as safe at home as any other place where some lunatic might track us."

"Okay." Rising to his feet, Zach lifted his hands in surrender. "I'll drive you home. Then, as a precaution, I'll ask Detective Gray to arrange for a female officer to spend the night with you."

The idea of a stranger in her home didn't feel all that reassuring. "Do you really think that's necessary?"

Zach's expression turned stern. "I won't take chances with your and Suzie's safety."

Tara stared at him, speechless, wondering why this seemed so personal to him. And why his protective reaction filled her with such a deep sense of reassurance. A feeling she could get used to. Which would be a colossal mistake.

Zach wasn't part of her life. He was just a man with a job to do.

Suzie dashed back into the room, a cupcake in each hand, her thumbs digging into the icing.

Zach relieved her of the goodies, and Suzie scrambled into Tara's lap before they could send her on another errand. Zach smiled over Suzie's head as he handed Tara a cupcake.

Reminded once more that her stomach still felt queasy, Tara set the cupcake on the table beside her.

Suzie snuggled under her arm. "I don't want to stay here, Mommy."

"You don't have to. Zach's offered to drive us home."

Mom appeared, carrying two cups of tea. "You're going?"

Hopeful it would settle her stomach, Tara gratefully accepted the cup. "After all the excitement, I think Suzie will sleep better in her own bed."

"Yes, I suppose that's true. If your father wasn't due home soon, I'd be tempted to leave with you."

Zach took the other teacup and offered Mom his hand. "Zach Reynolds. I'm an IT consultant at the hospital."

"Dak not a cop," Suzie chimed in.

"I can see that." Mom tousled Suzie's hair as she eyed Zach. "All the same, it's very nice of you to see Tara safely home."

A knock sounded and Suzie leaped from the chair.

"Let Grandma answer the door," Tara scolded.

Officer Nelson carried in Suzie's car seat, and Tara's purse and lunch bag. "I thought you might need these. The tow truck will be here shortly."

Mom bustled down the hall. "I'll get the vacuum and go over that car seat. Make sure no glass is left behind."

Suzie ran to the seat and poked her finger through a bullet hole in the plastic sidewall at head level. "Bad man hole my chair."

The blood drained from Tara's face and the room started to spin. Zach must've sprung to his feet and grabbed her tea, because the next thing she knew he was pushing her head to her knees.

"Breathe," he said gently. "It's okay. Suzie's okay. Take big breaths."

The air came in short gulps between snippets of horrible images of her baby being shot.

Zach rubbed her back. "Shh, it's okay."

Tara sprang upright. "How can you say that? My baby could've been killed."

He cupped his hands on her shoulders and forced her to look him in the eye. "She wasn't. And I'm going to make sure nothing happens to either of you. Understand?"

"Yes," she whispered, not ready to question how he planned to do that.

Thankfully, Mom distracted Suzie from Tara's meltdown by cajoling her into helping vacuum the safety seat.

As soon as they finished, Zach carried it to his truck.

"Who is that man?" Mom asked the instant the door closed behind him.

"Dak," Suzie piped up.

"Yes, sweetie." Mom rested her palm on Suzie's head and pinned her gaze on Tara. "How did he know you were here?"

"I was on the phone with him when the shots were fired."

"You're seeing him?"

"We're friends," Tara hedged. She'd known the man for twenty-four hours. It hardly qualified him as a friend, but telling Mom he was a cop wasn't an option. She'd scarcely explained how she'd injured her wrist last week let alone her suspicions about whoever had shoved her.

Mom looked as though she wanted to say more, but seemed to think better of it when Tara reached for Suzie.

By the time Tara had helped Suzie into her shoes and zipped up her ladybug jacket, her favorite, Zach had returned. He came through the back door. "The media is here. I've parked my truck at the neighbor's house behind this one. If we exit through the backyard, we won't be spotted." He turned to Tara's mother. "If they come to the door, perhaps you could say this has been quite a shock and your daughter is resting. That way they'll assume she's still here."

"Yes, I can do that."

He whisked Tara and Suzie outside, and within minutes they were headed back to Miller's Bay.

Tara gave him directions to her street, and then they lapsed into silence. As they passed the hospital, she said, "Why did you call me this afternoon?"

"I went looking for you to ask about your run-in with Whittaker. Nurse Bradshaw told me you went home sick."

"You heard about Whittaker?" She replayed in her mind their encounter outside the medicine locker. Did she really think he was capable of sweet-talking his patients into bequeathing their life's savings to the hospital, and then killing them to speed delivery?

Zach glanced at her, his forehead puckered. "I was there. Remember?"

"O-o-oh." She drew out the word to three syllables. "You're talking about the *first* incident."

His eyes widened. "What do you mean, *first?*"

Tara glanced over her shoulder at her ever-watchful daughter. "Perhaps we should talk about this later."

His gaze lifted to the rearview mirror. "Good idea." A few minutes later, he pulled into her driveway. "Wait here while I make sure it's safe."

"Um…" Her gaze darted from one window to the next. "I feel like a sitting duck. Don't you think it'd be safer if we all went in together?"

The muscle in his jaw twitched, telling her he didn't like the idea. He scanned the neighbors' yards and the street. "Okay, let's go."

By the time Tara had gathered her things and

climbed from the truck, Zach had Suzie unbuckled. He held out his palm. "Give me your keys."

With Suzie's safety paramount in her mind, she handed them over and took her daughter from his arms.

He unlocked the front door and hesitated as if bracing for an assault or explosion of some kind.

"What is it?"

He shook his head and moved inside. "Shut the door and wait here while I check the rest of the house."

The tender concern in his voice washed over her like a gentle rain, swishing away the tension that had knotted her stomach. She nudged a few pairs of tiny shoes out of his path. "Excuse the mess."

"You have a three-year-old. Messes go with the territory," he said, winking at her. "Nothing to apologize for."

His wink did funny things to her heart. Someone who didn't care about kids' messes might tempt her to reconsider her no-dating rule.

Right. She couldn't have picked a worse time to find herself attracted to a guy if she'd tried. And, boy, was she attracted.

She hugged Suzie tighter. Now was not the time to entertain such thoughts. Someone had shot at her tonight. Maybe intentionally.

Zach let his gaze skim over the living room and adjoining dining area. A poufy sofa and chair filled a couple of walls. A bookcase, its bottom shelves loaded with toys and picture books, adorned a third wall, and a large bay window encompassed the fourth. Recessed ceiling lights bathed the room in a warm glow. "Your place looks great. Homey."

Tara's lips curved into a smile that chased away the shadows around her eyes. "Thank you. That's the nicest thing anyone's ever said to me."

Uncertain how to respond, he ducked his head and murmured, "Stay put until I get back." He searched the two bedrooms, inspected the closets and under all the beds, and then checked the bathroom, kitchen and basement, assessing every window and door. Although reassured to find no evidence of an attempted break-in, he nevertheless put in a call to Rick.

Returning to the living room, he found Tara and Suzie sitting in an armchair, reading a picture book. The sight clogged his throat.

He coughed to clear it. "The place looks safe enough, so I went ahead and asked Detective Gray to send over a female officer to stay with you. I also ordered a pizza. I figured you might be hungry."

She fluttered her fingers through Suzie's hair. "I still don't feel up to eating, but I'm sure Suzie will appreciate it."

"Mmm," the little girl agreed, before scurrying over to her toy shelf.

Tara picked up her lunch bag and purse. "I guess I might as well chuck what's left of this macaroni salad." She opened the back door off the kitchen and scraped the contents from her container into the compost bucket.

"You need to eat something. Do you have crackers? They might settle your stomach."

She pulled a bag of soda crackers from the cupboard, plugged in the kettle for tea and then turned circles.

"Relax. Sit down," Zach said in the most soothing voice he could muster, considering what her restlessness was doing to him. "Tell me what happened with Whittaker."

"Oh." She placed her hands on the table, continuously clasping and unclasping her fingers. She must've noticed that the habit caught his attention, because she dropped her hands into her lap.

"Start by telling me why Whittaker grabbed your arm in the lobby."

"He said that I looked like I might faint or something."

Zach nudged the package of crackers toward her. "Did you feel faint?"

"More like shocked. I saw Mr. and Mrs. Parker's name on the donation wall. They didn't have that kind of money to donate. And…" Tara's explanation came out in a rush.

"Could've been a life-insurance policy. Since they both died the same day, the money would've gone to the beneficiaries of the estate. Or maybe, memorial gifts were made in their memory. I can check into it. It is a little suspicious."

"A *little?* Dr. Whittaker outright said to me that the less attention drawn to the Parkers' deaths, the better. So people wouldn't get the wrong idea."

"But he didn't imply that the deaths and the hospital's windfall were actually connected?"

Her voice rose a notch. "He implied that I'd better keep my mouth shut if I knew what was good for me."

"Whittaker actually threatened you?"

"Not in so many words. But don't you see? He must've charmed the Parkers into changing their will, and then bumped them off."

He quirked a brow. "Kind of a big risk for him to take when he doesn't personally benefit."

"Then who do you think it is?"

"I don't know, Tara. I don't know how killing a couple of terminally ill patients can score anyone a payoff."

Tara threw up her hands. "Why does it have to have anything to do with personal gain?"

"It doesn't. But it usually does."

"Well, that scratches the doctors." She sighed. "They can hardly be in need of more money."

"Not necessarily. Many graduate from med school with enormous financial debt."

The doorbell rang and Suzie sprang to her feet.

"No," Zach chided gently. "You mustn't open the door unless your mommy says it's okay." Heartened to see that being back in familiar surroundings had at least eradicated the youngster's fears, he glanced out the window. "It's Detective Gray and your pizza," he said to Tara.

"All right, Suzie. You can open the door this time. But next time, remember what Zach said—ask first."

Suzie's little legs scurried to the door in a blur that could outrace Wile E. Coyote.

"Well, hello," Rick's voice carried into the room. "Is your mommy home?"

Tara set her hands on Suzie's shoulders. "Come on in. Thanks for coming. And bringing supper."

"It's no trouble."

Tara leaned down and whispered in Suzie's ear, "You go wash your hands before we eat."

Suzie eyed Rick and the female officer curiously, then skedaddled down the hall.

Rick introduced the brunette at his side as Officer Kelly Teal, Tara's bodyguard for the evening. The attractive young officer wore jeans and a T-shirt and carried an overnight bag.

Tara gave Kelly an apologetic look. "I'm sure Zach's concerns are overblown. Officer Nelson was certain the shooting was a random gang thing."

Rick handed Tara the pizza box. "Let's pray so. In the meantime, Kelly will keep an eye out for any signs of trouble."

The kettle whistled. Tara let out a resigned sigh, set the pizza box on the coffee table and excused herself.

"What do you think?" Rick whispered to Zach as Kelly stowed her bag behind the sofa.

"No sign of anyone watching the place. The windows and doors have decent-enough locks. And, like she said, this could be a false alarm. Then again…"

Tara's scream split the air.

Zach rushed to the kitchen, Rick at his heels. The back screen door hung open. In the faint pool of light beyond the threshold, Tara stood frozen, her hand splayed over her throat, her gaze fixed on a convulsing baby raccoon.

Suzie darted into the room, but Kelly immediately corralled her into the living room. Zach clasped Tara's upper arms from behind and urged her back inside.

She whirled to face him and his heart wrenched. She'd gone ashen, her eyes glazed, her body trembling. It was all he could do not to fold her in his arms.

He spotted the upturned compost bucket and shot a glance to Rick.

"What was in that bucket?" Rick asked.

"My leftover lunch." Tara choked on the words as her terrified eyes met Zach's. "Someone tried to poison me."

FOUR

Detective Gray's voice registered faintly in Tara's churning mind. He cupped his hands over her shoulders. "We need to get you to the hospital and have you checked."

"We can't take her to Memorial," Zach said.

Tara's breaths came in short gasps. *Someone tried to poison me!*

She gripped the edge of the counter, forcing herself to inhale deeply as she waited for the room to stop spinning.

"She needs an ambulance, *now,*" Detective Gray barked.

"No, I don't think I ingested enough to—"

"I'll take her to Hamilton," Zach said, cutting off her argument. "We don't want whoever did this to know we're onto them."

"I can stay here with your daughter if you like," chirped the female cop assigned to be Tara's bodyguard.

Feeling like a child at the mercy of grown-ups determined to make the decision for her, Tara looked from Detective Gray's grim face to Zach's.

"You need to be checked," Zach said softly.

Tara nodded. He was right, of course. But she hated being the patient. She returned to the living room, her gaze shifting to the inky blackness outside. Whoever had done this to her could be out there even now. Watching her.

She yanked the drapes closed, then kneeled in front of Suzie playing with her toys. Tara's heart raced. She didn't know the female officer. Could she trust her alone with her daughter? Did she dare, when a killer clearly wanted to silence her?

"Honey, Mommy needs to go back to the hospital for a little while. Would you like to come?"

Suzie rubbed her eyes with tiny fists. "No. Don't wanna."

"Would you like Miss Kelly to stay here with you, then?"

Suzie's gaze darted from Kelly to Zach. "Want Dak."

The female officer chuckled.

Zach hunkered down in front of Suzie. "I'd like that, but I can't this time. Your mom needs me to drive her to the hospital. Kelly will take good care of you. Okay?"

Tara's heart clenched at the disappointment that clouded Suzie's eyes. She pulled her into a warm hug. "I won't be long. I'm sure if you ask, Kelly will read you lots of stories."

"Oh, I love to read stories," Kelly gushed.

"O-kay," Suzie said, with enough reluctance in her voice to heap up the guilt Tara battled every time she had to leave her daughter in someone else's care.

Zach rose. "Come on. The sooner we get you looked at, the sooner you'll be back."

Detective Gray emerged from the kitchen with her lunch container. "I'll have this dusted for fingerprints and tested for poison. Who had access to your lunch?"

An involuntary shiver trembled through her entire body. She tightened her hold on Suzie, shutting down the thought of how differently this day could've turned out.

Suzie squirmed.

Tara loosened her hold and sat back on her heels. For her daughter's sake, she fought to keep her voice even. "I put my lunch in the staff-lounge fridge when I got to work."

"I'll need a list of everyone who might've accessed that fridge."

"Dozens of people have access. Housekeeping staff, doctors, nurses. Sometimes we even let the spouses of our long-term patients use the fridge." A lump swelled in Tara's throat. What was she saying? How could one of her coworkers try to kill her?

Blackness crept into the edge of her vision. She caught the corner of the coffee table.

Zach cupped her elbow. "Easy." He coaxed her to her feet. "Come on. We need to get going. You can jot down names as I drive."

Tara took a fortifying breath and gave Suzie one last squeeze. "Be good for Kelly, okay?"

Already absorbed in her play, Suzie merely nodded.

Tara rushed out to Zach's truck before she could change her mind about letting Suzie stay behind. Zach quickly corralled her inside, shielding her from the road with his body and scanning every hedge and tree where a shooter might hide. Once inside the truck, he flipped on the dome light and handed her a notepad and pencil, his expression so sympathetic she had to look away.

He pulled onto the road. "Tell me about Suzie's father."

"Why?" Tara's heart pinched. Wasn't it bad enough she'd been shot at and poisoned? Did he have to pry into the humiliation of her failed marriage, too?

"We've assumed the attacks are connected to the deaths at the hospital, but we need to consider all the possibilities."

Tara squared her jaw. "I haven't seen my husband since he walked out on us."

"He hasn't stayed in touch? Not even to see Suzie?"

"No." Last week's two-line note asking if he could drop by—three years too late—could hardly be considered staying in touch. "His lawyer served the divorce papers, and Earl surrendered all custodial rights." He'd remarried, and if the grapevine could be believed, his wife was infertile. The Earl she knew would've been fine with that, which had made his sudden attempt to reconnect all the more strange.

"I see," Zach said through gritted teeth. "You deserve better."

Tara's heart gave a little kick at the fervency behind his words. Everyone had always loved Earl—his friendly, outgoing charm. No one had ever told her that *she* deserved better. *No one.*

"What about neighbors? Former colleagues? Former boyfriends? Can you think of anyone who might have a vendetta against you?"

"No. Well…I suppose a patient's loved one might. Sometimes relatives blame medical personnel after a family member's death."

"Any patient in particular?"

Tara peered into the darkness. "No, none that I can think of."

"You mentioned that Alice had a grudge against you. Do you think she could've done this?"

"Alice?" Tara's voice rose at the ludicrousness of the idea. "She wants me demoted. Not dead."

"You never know what someone is capable of."

The image of the convulsing baby raccoon spiraled across Tara's vision. Her stomach roiled. What if she'd fed her lunch leftovers to Suzie?

She shoved the pad and pencil to the floor and grabbed the door handle. "Pull over."

Zach stomped on the brake.

Tara shot from the truck and heaved. *Oh, God, why are You letting this happen to us? I tried to do what was right, and now some psycho is coming after me. How can I protect my baby?*

Zach raced to her side, patted her back. "You okay?"

She flung out her arm, knocking away his hand. "Do I *look* okay? Someone tried to kill me!"

"Yes, and you're angry. But please know that we'll do everything in our power to keep you safe."

That was more than she could hope for from God. She wiped her mouth and tramped back to the truck.

Zach started to follow, then stopped, his attention riveted to the road behind them.

Tara spun in her seat, the *tick-tick* of the hazard lights reverberating through her chest.

The car behind them slowed to a crawl, then sped past.

A gawker? Or someone following them?

Zach whipped out his cell phone and made a quick call before returning to the driver's side.

"Who was that?" Tara blurted the moment he opened the door.

"Probably no one. But I called in the license plate and told Rick to run extra patrols past your place."

"You think this guy's watching my house?"

Zach veered back onto the road and punched off the hazards. "Anything's possible, Tara. It would be safer if you got out of town for a while."

"I can't. I already told you that."

"Your safety, not to mention your daughter's, is more important than a promotion."

"Don't you think I know that? I am not some money-grubbing workaholic—I'm a single mom. If I want to keep my daughter clothed and fed, I need this job."

Not to mention she needed to avoid giving Earl any leverage, in case a desire to reclaim custody was behind his recent contact.

"Okay." Zach didn't bother tempering the exasperation in his voice. "But tomorrow, you call in sick. The attacks have all been centered at the hospital, even the shooting, if it's connected. With the weekend and your regular day off Monday, that'll give me four days to flush this guy out. With any luck, he'll assume he managed to scare you off."

Tara could only pray he was right.

The next day, Zach wasn't sure what would've been less distracting—having Tara at the hospital or spending the day worrying about who might be terrorizing her. The investigating officer had no leads on the shooter. Rick had managed to recover one usable thumbprint from the lunch container, but it didn't match any in the database. And an unknown enemy was the most difficult to defend against. What kind of monster laced a young mother's lunch with arsenic?

Zach shook off a surge of anger and forced his attention to the computer in front of him. He couldn't afford to let his emotions get in the way. Last night Tara and her little girl had invaded his dreams, muddled with memories of his late wife.

He'd been prepared for those flashbacks. Spending time in a cancer ward again, they'd been inevitable.

He could handle them. Tara and Suzie, he wasn't so sure about.

He inserted his pass card into the nurses' station computer and tuned in to the conversations around him.

Alice Bradshaw stopped at the desk and picked up a file. A teenage volunteer, pushing a cart of paperbacks and newspapers, halted at her side. "Miss Clark had a friend over, too, but he left before the ambulance got there. Weird, huh?"

Zach zeroed in on the nurse to gauge her reaction. Were they talking about Ellen Clark, the most recent alleged victim of their phantom killer?

"How do you know she had a friend over?"

"My Gran lives in the apartment next door. She heard someone just before the paramedics showed up."

"You shouldn't talk about this here," Alice reprimanded. "You'll upset the patients. Some of them knew Ellen."

Zach's fingers stilled over the keyboard. So they were talking about the victim.

The pair headed up the hall. "I'm just saying," the teen continued, "what kind of friend calls an ambulance for you and then splits?"

Good question. He pulled out his cell phone and texted Rick—*Need report on Ellen Clark's 9-1-1 call.* Zach mentally reviewed what he knew about the woman. Single, thirty-five, she'd been hospitalized three times in the past year.

Rick rang back immediately. "The call came from

Clark's home phone. Male voice. The message was 'A woman's seizing. Send an ambulance.'"

Yes! They were finally getting somewhere.

"What's the significance?"

"The caller scrammed before the ambulance got there." Zach scanned the vicinity and lowered his voice. "We could have a voiceprint of the killer."

"Why would a killer call for an ambulance? Never mind. It doesn't matter. Ellen Clark died from natural causes—an infection. I got the coroner's report this afternoon."

"The coroner said the same thing about Debra Parker." Yesterday Zach would've jumped on the excuse to shelve this investigation, but not after the attacks against Tara. "This guy's disappearance begs the question—why didn't he want to be seen at Ellen Clark's apartment?"

A loud smack snapped Zach's focus from the computer to the hallway. "I gotta go." He snapped shut his phone and rounded the doorway of the nurse's station to see what was going on.

A male in jeans and a disheveled shirt, mid-twenties, face twisted in pain, slapped his palm against the wall.

"Hey, you okay?"

The guy, eyes red-rimmed, stared blankly at Zach for a second before answering. "Yeah. Just peachy." Muttering to himself, he paced several feet down the hall, turned, paced back, turned again.

Deciding the guy's problem wasn't physical, Zach backed off. But he'd seen enough desperation in his career to want to keep an eye on him. At the moment, the hallway was empty, and the guy was a lightweight, no more than five-ten. If he started doing more than slap a few walls, Zach figured he could handle him.

The next time the guy turned, he covered his head with his hands and slumped heavily against the wall. With an anguished moan, he slid to the floor as if his legs couldn't hold him up. With his knees crunched to his chest, he banged the back of his head against the wall.

Zach rushed to his side. "Hey, buddy. Do you need a nurse?"

The guy jerked away from Zach's touch. Dropping his arms from over his head, he stared at the opposite wall. "No, I need a priest."

Zach offered him a wry grin. "Sorry, not my specialty."

The guy looked at him a moment, and then one side of his mouth quirked up a fraction. "I'm okay. Just thought if a pastor was handy I could convince my fiancée to marry me."

Confused, Zach looked around. Then understanding dawned. "She's a cancer patient?"

The man's shoulders sank four inches with the breath that whooshed from his chest. "Yeah. And I don't know what to do."

Zach urged him to his feet and ushered him to a chair. "Tell me what happened."

The young man hung his head. "Melanie's not responding to treatment."

Muffling a groan, Zach pulled up a chair beside him. "I'm sorry to hear that."

"And now she says she doesn't want to marry me. She says it wouldn't be fair."

"Fair to who?"

"That's what *I* said. No one comes with guarantees. I could be hit by a truck driving home." This time, when the guy met Zach's gaze, he had fire in his eyes. The fire of youth—bold, impetuous and naive. "What matters is that I love her."

"Enough to hold her head over the toilet while she pukes her guts out?" Zach felt compelled to ask, even though the shadows circling the young man's eyes and the worry lines lashed across his brow said he did.

"I'd do anything I could to make this miserable disease easier on her."

Memories of anguished prayers and endless bedside vigils whispered through Zach's mind, wrenching the breath from his lungs. He knew this man's lament too well. He wouldn't wish it on anyone. *Lord, show me what to say, how to comfort.*

"Mel read about some promising treatments at a clinic in Mexico. She wants to go. I asked her to marry me right away so we can go together."

"What'd she say?"

"She cried. Then she asked me to leave so she could talk to the doctor alone."

Zach laid his hand on the man's shoulder. "That's not a no."

The man hunched forward and gripped his head in his hands.

Zach squelched the urge to say more. Now was not the time to explain that his fiancée was grieving for all the things she might never have—like the fairytale wedding every girl dreams of. Compelled to reach out in some small way, Zach said, "May I meet Melanie?" The man scrubbed at his eyes and looked at him hopefully. Dr. McCrae stepped out of a room down the hall, and the young man jumped to his feet. "Yes, come on."

Zach braced himself as he followed the man into the room.

A frail young woman with hollow cheeks and sparse blond hair sat in the bed, a computer on her lap. "Jeff!" She beckoned her fiancé closer. "Dr. McCrae told me about alternative-treatment clinics here in Canada. Come see."

A zing of respect for the resident raised Zach's opinion of him a notch. In his experience, M.D.'s rarely spoke favorably about alternative therapies.

Jeff took Melanie's hand, his face mirroring her hopeful expression. "But I thought the treatment you wanted to try wasn't available here."

Wanting to give them privacy, Zach backed toward the door.

Melanie glanced up. "Who are you?"

"Oh, sorry." Jeff waved Zach toward the bed. "This is…"

"Zach." He extended his hand. "You must be

Melanie—the gorgeous fiancée that I've heard so much about."

Pink tinged her cheeks.

Jeff perched on the side of Melanie's bed and cradled her arm to his chest. "She sure is." The cell phone on his hip buzzed. He checked the screen. "My boss. Sorry, I have to take this. I'll be back in a few minutes."

Jeff left Zach standing at the foot of Melanie's bed. "Your fiancé's a great guy," he said.

A sad smile dimmed the hope that had been in her eyes when he entered the room. "Yes."

"He told me you were having second thoughts about getting married."

She closed her computer. "He shouldn't have. That's between us."

"He was upset. It was either talk to me or get escorted out of the building for beating up the wall."

Melanie's sheepish expression turned to a genuine smile.

"You know, we guys aren't as tough as we like others to think. When it comes to the women we love, we're soft as marshmallows." She giggled and Zach pressed his advantage. "When someone we love is hurting, we need to make ourselves useful, or we go nuts. We want to be the hero, the protector. It's what we do." He shrugged with a go-figure expression. "I know you love Jeff or you wouldn't try to shield him from your pain." Zach let his tone grow more serious. "But believe me, the best way to love him is to let him be here for you, no matter what."

Tears glistened in her eyes.

A moment later, Jeff returned.

Zach gave Melanie a wink. "Nice meeting you."

He returned to the nurse's station with a prayer for Melanie's well-being on his heart. His mind immediately veered back to Tara. And for the thousandth time since hearing the gunshots shatter her car window, he prayed for her safety.

His cell phone vibrated, alerting him to an incoming message.

His pulse spiked at the sight of the bodyguard's name and a terse message. *Call me. Urgent.*

Zach dialed the number and descended the back stairs two at a time. "What's wrong?"

"Not sure anything is. Yet. A floral delivery truck just pulled into the driveway. The driver is heading to the door with an arrangement as we speak. Did you send it?"

"Me? No!" Tara was a witness. Nothing more. He didn't want to consider why Kelly would think otherwise.

"Okay. Just checking." The sound of a doorbell chimed in the background. "So what do you want me to do? Tara says no one ever sends her flowers."

Zach raced to his truck, forcing a calm into his voice he didn't feel. "Leave the delivery outside—as far away from the house as you can discreetly manage. I'll be right there."

FIVE

At the sound of tires screeching to a stop in her driveway, Tara rushed to the window and nudged aside the curtain. Zach must have run every stop sign in town to get here this fast. Why hadn't Kelly called him back once they'd learned the flowers were from Mom's neighbor?

Tara looked at the note card the cautious detective had pulled from the floral arrangement, and stroked the ladybug pendant adorning the corner. Mom must've told Mr. Calloway how crazy Suzie was about ladybugs. The card said simply, *Hope you're feeling better.*

But, judging by the grim look on Zach's face as Kelly pointed him toward the backyard where she'd stashed the delivery, he wasn't convinced the sender was sincere.

Tara dropped the note card on the dining table next to the photos she'd been sorting and spied out the kitchen window.

From the way Zach examined each flower, paying extra attention to the center of a black-eyed Susan, he wasn't taking any chances. Next he scrutinized the pouch of plant food taped to the stems.

What was he thinking? Was there a substance that exploded on contact with water? Or that gave off a toxic gas?

Tara tensed. This threat might be a false alarm, but if Zach feared her assailant could take her out with a bouquet of flowers, how did he ever expect to keep her safe?

A few moments later, Zach followed Kelly back inside and presented Tara with the bouquet. "For you."

His fingers grazed hers, and her heart squeezed with a sudden irrational disappointment that the flowers weren't from him. Averting her gaze, she mumbled her thanks.

"Dak here!" Suzie squealed and scurried toward him, dragging her puppet.

Zach's mouth stretched into a smile almost as wide as the puppet's. "Hey, kiddo. What you got there?"

"Micah." She shoved the orange-haired dummy into Zach's hand. "Talk."

"You're supposed to be taking a nap," Tara admonished.

Zach gave Tara a wink and slipped on the puppet.

His sweet way with Suzie triggered another unexpected pang in the vicinity of her heart. But no matter how nice he seemed, she couldn't let Suzie get too attached. He was here to do a job. And when it was finished, he'd be gone.

Imitating a yawn, Zach patted the puppet's hand to

its mouth. "I'm tired," he said in a squeaky voice, his lips unmoving. "I wanna finish my nap."

Suzie laughed and hugged Micah to her chest. "Me, too. Let's go, Micah."

When Suzie dashed back to her bedroom without making a fuss, Tara blinked in astonishment. "How'd you do that?"

Zach shrugged. "Standard police tactic. Make them think they want to do the right thing."

Tara laughed. "I'll have to remember that." She pulled a vase from the cupboard and arranged the flowers. "Will you stay for a coffee?"

"That's okay. I'm sure you want to take advantage of Suzie's nap time to get your own stuff done."

"No, I want to hear what you've uncovered."

Zach sank into a kitchen chair and rattled off what little he knew. "We'll analyze the voiceprint on the 9-1-1 call, rule out thumbprints of hospital staff, cross-reference staff schedules to the time of the incidents." He took a breath. "If your shooter and poisoner are the same person, he had to have been in before lunch, then clocked out early enough to follow you from the hospital."

"What about the Parkers' donation? Did you learn anything more about that?"

"I confirmed that it wasn't a memorial gift in their honor. Rick's working on getting a warrant to see their will."

She sighed heavily. "So what am I supposed to do in the meantime?"

"You stay put. I'll keep looking." Zach picked up a photo from the table. "I didn't know you run."

"Yeah, a couple of marathons and some shorter races."

"Any serious rivalry between competitors we should know about?" Kelly interjected.

"Hardly. I always finish in the bottom half."

Zach gazed at her with an admiration that left her skin tingly. "Hey, I'm impressed by anyone who can finish such a grueling race."

She rolled her eyes and returned to scooping ground coffee.

"I'm serious. I've tried running a couple of marathons, but never finished. Maybe we could run together sometime. You could give me some tips."

Her heart gave a silly little skip, but she wasn't willing to admit how much the idea appealed to her. Aside from races, she'd never run with anyone other than Suzie in the racing buggy. And if she didn't want Suzie getting hurt, she'd better keep it that way.

By Monday afternoon, Tara wished she'd taken Zach up on his offer to go running.

She rotated three hundred and sixty degrees, glancing from one draped window to the next. This was ridiculous. She shoved aside the front curtains. Then strode to the kitchen window and snapped open the blinds.

The sun was shining. The trees were ablaze with color and the mercury had topped sixty-five. Perfect running weather. And after being cooped up inside for the past three and a half days, she had energy to burn.

She refused to be a prisoner in her own house a second longer.

Detective Gray wouldn't have pulled Kelly off guard duty if he'd still been worried about Tara's safety outside the hospital.

She scooped her hair into a ponytail and pulled on her sneakers. "Hey, Suzie, let's go for a run."

Suzie sprang to her feet, toppling the toy animals from her lap. Her little hands fisted, and she jogged on the spot. "Run."

"That's right, but you get to ride." Tara pulled a lightweight hoodie over the child's head and kissed her nose. "Okay?"

"Okay," Suzie squealed, and ran to the garage where they kept the racing stroller.

By the time Tara locked the side door, Suzie had climbed into the buggy and was smushing the two buckle ends together in a hopeless attempt to snap herself in.

Smiling indulgently at her daughter, Tara snapped the ends together, pushed the timer on her watch and headed left out of the driveway.

"Wrong way," Suzie shouted over the wind whooshing past the stroller.

"We're taking a different route today." *Just in case.*

Two miles out, she realized her mistake. Anyone who knew her routine wouldn't expect to find her jogging down Vine Street, but everything on the street was unfamiliar. She had no sense whether someone was lurking where he shouldn't be. She glanced over her shoulder. Maybe she should've asked Zach to join her. One look at his big, muscular arms and no one would try to mess with her. For a few strides, she let herself imagine what it would be like to be held in those arms—safe from shadowy threats.

She squashed the thought. Even if she were interested in dating again—which she *wasn't*—he'd only be in town for a few weeks, tops. Then he'd be gone.

Five miles out, her heart raced faster than normal. Sweat prickled her skin. She glanced from side to side, and then behind her, once again. Instead of feeling relaxed, she felt jumpier than before she'd started. When a kid swooped past her on a bicycle, she actually yelped.

At Elm, she turned west. The canopy of trees cast long shadows over the yards where anyone might be lurking. Waiting.

Fallen leaves crackled beneath the wheels of the buggy, making it difficult to hear anything else. She caught sight of another jogger out of her peripheral— a guy, Whittaker's height, ball cap pulled low over his eyes.

He rounded the corner, closed the gap between them.

Suddenly the crackling leaves became deafening. Or maybe it was the blood roaring past her ears.

She stepped up her pace.

So did he.

* * *

Why wasn't Tara answering her door?

Zach fisted his hand and pounded louder. Nothing. He jiggled the knob without success. Whipping out his phone, he scanned the windows for signs of movement. The sound of Tara's telephone penetrated the walls, but inside no one moved toward the phone. He tried Kelly's.

"Detective Teal."

"Where are you?" he barked.

"Didn't Gray tell you?"

"Tell me what?"

"He pulled me off guard duty a couple of hours ago. You know how it goes. The budget—"

"He *what?*" Zach tried to stay calm. "I don't believe this. Where is she now?"

"At home. At least she was when I left two hours ago."

"Did she mention her plans? Errands she had to run, maybe?"

"No."

Tamping down his fear, Zach snapped shut his phone. Tara's car—the window repaired—sat in the driveway. Shutting down visions of her and Suzie being abducted, he checked the garage. Sure enough, Suzie's stroller was missing. It was such a nice day. Tara had likely walked her daughter to the park.

Zach jumped into his truck and trolled the neighborhood. After a few blocks, he widened the net and wound his way through the surrounding subdivisions.

He turned onto Chestnut Lane. Majestic trees shaded the street, and prestigious-looking turn-of-the-century homes with manicured lawns graced either side. Must be where the doctors and lawyers lived.

But there was no sign of Tara and Suzie.

Zach took the first left. A playground occupied the next corner. *Bingo.*

Sunbeams blinded him as he rounded the bend. Then a woman pushing a racing buggy burst from the shadows. Tara.

She tossed a glance over her shoulder, and her look of sheer panic kicked him in the gut.

An instant later, a man in a ball cap appeared. The man's strides lengthened, chewing the distance between them.

Heart pounding, Zach punched the gas. But before he could intercept, the runner overtook Tara, shooting her an odd look as he passed.

Tara stopped dead in her tracks.

Zach swerved to the curb and jumped out of his truck. "Are you okay?"

In the buggy, Suzie slept peacefully. Tara spun toward him, wild-eyed.

His heart rate kicked up another notch.

Relief washed over her face, and for an instant, she looked like she might fling herself into his arms. Instead, she hunched forward, pinched her sides, and gulped in air.

He took a step back, swallowing his disappointment and giving his own pulse a moment to slow. He squinted at the runner disappearing in the distance. "What happened? Who was that guy?"

"I thought, I thought—" She sucked in breaths one on top of the other. Perspiration trickled down her cheek. "I thought he was chasing me." She swiped at her face with the back of her hand and glanced over her shoulder.

"Did you recognize him?"

She shook her head. She paced, and her breathing began to slow. "I couldn't see his face."

Zach let out a pent-up breath. Part of him wanted to take off after the guy. But the guy had looked like he was just trying to run past her, and had probably felt challenged when she'd picked up her pace.

Tara's gaze skittered across the horizon, and her flushed cheeks deepened a shade. She stopped pacing and wrapped her arms around her middle. "I guess I got kind of spooked."

He slipped his arm across her shoulder and gave her a sideways hug. "Hey, if you think a bad guy's chasing you, I'd rather see you run than give him the benefit of the doubt."

Her chuckle resonated through his chest. He dropped his arm, unnerved by how right she felt there. "Why don't we sit in the park for a few minutes? I can fill you in on what I learned today." He steered the buggy toward a bench. "Sweet rig. You can really move."

"Thanks." Her lips curved into a self-deprecating smile. "I think."

Relieved to see her playful sense of humor reemerging, he parked the buggy in front of the bench and invited Tara to take a seat.

"I need to shake out a bit first, or I'll pay for it later."

Zach averted his gaze from the shapely muscles sculpting her legs and focused on her sleeping daughter. "Does Suzie usually fall asleep when you run?"

"Yes, it's a mixed blessing. Nap times at home are when I try to catch up on paperwork." She made a face that said paperwork ranked right up there with cleaning toilets on her list of favorite things to do.

Zach laughed.

Suzie startled at the sound. Her mouth opened as if she might cry, but when her gaze met his, she let out a squeal instead. "Dak!"

His heart swelled. "Hi, there, Suzie." He unzipped the windbreak covering the buggy, unhooked the buckle and lifted her out. "How's my favorite girl?"

She beamed at Tara as if she thought her mom should answer. The notion made Zach's heart skip a beat. When had he stopped wanting to solve this case and get out of town ASAP? Now it seemed he wanted to stay here, or more precisely, he wanted an excuse to keep seeing Tara and Suzie, as he'd done daily for the past four days.

Tara tapped Suzie's nose. "Suzie's been a good girl today."

"Good girl." Suzie squirmed for release.

Zach looked to Tara for permission, and at her nod, let Suzie race for the playground.

Tara pulled the elastic from her hair and turned her

head from side to side. The breeze swished the stray strands from her shoulder, rousing a faint lavender scent that teased Zach's senses.

He redirected his focus to Suzie as she scrambled up the ladder of the kiddie slide. "We got a look at the Parkers' will. Mr. Parker had a sizable life-insurance policy. Since the Parkers had no children, they bequeathed their entire estate to the hospital."

"I told you Whittaker was behind this."

Zach had spent the weekend trailing Whittaker between the golf course, his home, and evening parties, and hadn't seen a hint of anything suspicious. "We have no proof. We've already ruled out his thumbprint as a match."

Tara sank onto the bench beside him. "He could've worn gloves."

"The man had nothing to gain that we can see from the Parkers' deaths. Not personally. And the donation to the hospital was hardly substantial enough to motivate him to risk his career, let alone his freedom." Zach gripped the edge of the seat to resist the impulse to give Tara's hand a reassuring squeeze. "We'll find the guy, Tara. I promise you."

Suzie skipped toward them and patted Zach's knee. "You're it," she squealed, racing away.

Zach chased after her, pretending to slip and slide around the playground equipment in a desperate attempt to catch her. At Tara's sweet laughter, he changed course and tapped her arm. "You're it." He grinned and darted out of her reach.

"Catch me. Catch me, Mommy." Suzie bounced up and down on the platform above the slide.

Tara scrambled up the ladder after her.

Suzie zoomed down the slide and took him out at the bottom.

"Here I come." Tara charged down the slide after her little girl.

Halfway to his feet, Zach caught Suzie and Tara in a giant bear hug. "Ha! I got you both."

"You're not it," Suzie protested.

Tara tapped his shoulder. "Now he is."

Since his arms were occupied, he gave Suzie a peck on the forehead. "You're it."

She patted him back. "You are. Kiss Mommy, kiss Mommy."

When Tara's laughter-filled gaze met his, he couldn't resist. He shifted Suzie to his hip and, curling his arm, pulled Tara to his other side. Time slowed. She smelled of sunshine and adventure. He lowered his head and she tried to squirm free. But deciding her attempts were more feigned than real, he brushed his lips softly against hers, lingering long enough to whisper, "You're it."

Her lips stretched into a smile beneath his.

Oh, wow. They stepped apart, and Tara looked as stunned as he felt.

"Um…" She cast her gaze about the playground. "I'd better get Suzie home. It's almost suppertime."

"I'll give you a lift," Zach said quickly, not ready to let her go. "I can put the buggy in the back."

"Yay!" Suzie raced for his truck before Tara had a chance to object.

Zach grabbed the buggy while Tara gave chase. He'd been stupid to kiss her. Stupid. Stupid. Stupid.

The short drive to the house was uncomfortably quiet. Excited as she'd been, Suzie drifted to sleep the moment the truck started moving.

Tara felt Suzie's forehead. "She must be coming down with something."

"You unlock the house and I'll carry her in for you." As Zach backed out of the rear of the cab with Suzie in his arms, Tara gasped.

"Put her back inside the truck," she hissed.

A dark-haired man in black jeans and a black polo shirt stepped into view.

"Do you know this man?"

"Yes, he's my ex. Put Suzie back in the truck. Please." She met the guy halfway up the walk.

Zach did as Tara asked.

The guy stuffed a pen and paper into his jacket pocket. "Tara, good to see you. I was just going to leave you a note."

Tara visibly stiffened.

Zach strode to her side. "May I help you?"

The man was clean-shaven, a shade gaunt, but not bad-looking. He snubbed his nose at Zach's question and returned his attention to Tara. "Who's the bodyguard?"

"He's just a friend."

The title stung. As much as he knew he shouldn't be

thinking it, that kiss had made him wish they'd moved beyond friendship, had made him think that he might be ready to move on from Carole's death.

"Zach, this is Earl."

Zach shook the man's hand with an extra-firm grip, then dug his fists into his pockets. The other night, she'd made it sound as though her ex was out of the picture. Clearly, he wasn't.

Earl's gaze skimmed Tara's body with obvious appreciation. "You're looking good. Still running, I see."

"What do you want?"

His hands shot up, all innocence. "Hey, can't a man visit his wife and kid?"

"Ex-wife. And since when do you care about our daughter?"

Earl's gaze cut to Zach, as if to say his reasons were private.

Zach backed toward the truck. "Maybe I should go," he said, although he had no intention of leaving this dirtbag alone with Tara.

"No need. Earl's not staying."

"Just give me five minutes," Earl pleaded. "Five minutes."

Tara nodded to Zach to give them a moment alone. Her gaze shifted nervously toward Suzie, before she led her ex inside.

Reluctantly, Zach retreated to the truck, where he whipped out his phone and dialed Rick. "I need you to do a background check on Earl Peterson."

"Tara's ex?"

"Yeah, he showed up unannounced at her house." Zach noticed an overturned flowerpot and a dent in the flower bed where a rock or something had recently sat. "Looks like he tried to get in."

A neighbor in the next yard eyed Zach curiously.

He cupped his hand around the phone so he couldn't be overheard. "Tara hasn't seen this guy in three years. Why's he suddenly back in town? I don't like it."

"Okay. I'll see what I can find out."

Pocketing his phone, Zach scanned the street. No car sat parked at the curb. Clearly, Earl hadn't wanted her to see him coming. What might he have done if he'd found Tara at home?

Through the living-room window, Zach saw Earl carry a ladder out of the kitchen and follow Tara down the hall toward the bedrooms. He didn't like this. He didn't like this at all. But clearly Tara didn't want Earl seeing Suzie, and Zach wasn't about to leave the little girl alone in the truck.

A few minutes later, Zach spotted Earl and Tara heading toward the front door.

Zach met them at the porch.

"Did you want to meet Suzie before you go?" Tara asked her ex, although the offer sounded forced.

Earl slanted a wistful glance toward the truck. "That's okay, it'll only confuse the kid." He held up the shoe box he'd apparently come for. "See you around."

Zach cringed at the suggestion. The first thing he planned to do when he left here tonight was buy new locks for Tara's doors. He waited until Earl had sauntered down the street before scooping Suzie from the backseat and rejoining Tara on the porch. "What did he want?"

"Some stuff he'd stored in the attic. I didn't even know it was there."

Suspicions needled the back of Zach's neck. "What kind of stuff?"

"Nothing important." Waving off his concern, she moved inside. "His old baseball cards and comic books. He lost his job and hopes to cash in on the collection."

The thought of her ex nosing around here for something to hock rankled. "Did you change the locks after your divorce?"

"Yes."

"Glad to hear it. Do you mind if I check the attic? Make sure he didn't leave anything behind?"

"What do you mean?" Her eyes widened. "You mean like spy equipment?"

Yeah. But he just shrugged.

"You think Earl's the one who poisoned—?" Her voice edged higher.

"No. He would've been noticed."

"Then, what?"

"Maybe he wants his daughter back."

"He didn't even want to see her!" Tara reached for Suzie, and as she clutched the sleeping child to her chest, something inside him shifted.

"I'm sorry, Tara. It's just a precaution." Although

Zach hadn't missed the hint of yearning in Earl's glance toward Suzie.

Tara let out a weary sigh and headed toward Suzie's room. "Do whatever you need to do."

Standing atop the ladder, Zach scanned the attic with his penlight. Aside from the flattened place where the shoe box must have sat, none of the insulation appeared disturbed. He slipped out to his truck for his fingerprint kit, and then dusted the ladder and the attic hatch. He doubted Earl's thumbprint would match the one lifted from Tara's lunch container, but having Earl's prints on file might prove useful.

Because Zach had a bad feeling they hadn't seen the last of the man.

SIX

Still running, I see. Her ex-husband's pointed remark replayed in Tara's mind as she ran through the rain from the parking lot to the hospital. She stopped under the awning and shook the water from her jacket. Why wouldn't he get out of her head?

Still running.

As if she had much choice, with a daughter to raise alone. Not that that's what he'd meant. But after nursing Suzie through a high fever most of the night and then racing around this morning to make alternative child-care arrangements, she felt as though she hadn't stopped running since that magical moment Zach had caught her at the bottom of the slide.

Her fingers went to her lips as the memory of his kiss washed over her anew. He'd tasted minty fresh, like sunshine after a storm.

Stop thinking about him.

She headed for the nurses' locker room. As soon as they solved the Parkers' murders, Zach would leave. Dreaming about more kisses was pointless. And if that weren't reason enough to ignore the silly flutter in her chest every time she thought about him, seeing Earl should have been. Once upon a time, his kisses had tilted her world, too.

But the final kiss-off had left it permanently out of whack.

She threw her purse into her locker and slammed the door. The metal clattered.

Of course, unlike Zach, Earl didn't adore children and had zero tolerance for their messes. And not once had he come to her defense, not even when Mom or one of her sisters had ragged on her. Whereas Zach seemed to be protecting her at every turn. He must have even bullied Detective Gray into sending extra patrols past the house. She'd counted no less than four pass by between midnight and three, when Suzie's fever finally broke.

As much as Tara wanted to never depend on a guy again, she had to admit that having someone look out for her for a change felt kind of nice.

Distracted by her thoughts, Tara almost plowed into Kim outside the locker room. "Kim, what are you doing here?"

They'd rekindled their childhood friendship when Kim's father was hospitalized earlier in the year. But since her engagement, the youth worker had been busy planning her wedding and helping her fiancé take over her father's role as director of Hope Manor.

"I had to escort a resident from the detention center for some tests and wanted to pop down to say hi. I'm afraid that I've been neglecting my friends."

"Well, it's not every day a girl gets married, so I forgive you."

Kim squealed. "Can you believe it? Only seven more weeks."

Tara squeezed Kim's hand. "I'm so happy for you. Do you have time for a coffee? My shift doesn't start for a few minutes yet."

"Sure, my partner can handle the resident's supervision alone for a bit longer."

Tara led the way to the staff lounge. As she passed staff she hadn't seen since the poisoned-lunch incident, her stomach tightened. Zach had said to act as if nothing had happened, as if she'd just been off with the flu. But their curious stares made her skin prickle and her legs turn wooden.

She ducked into the lounge and came face-to-face with Dr. Whittaker.

Instinctively, she recoiled. If Kim hadn't been behind her, who knew what she would've said or done next?

He wore a flattering purple shirt and tie with a stethoscope draped around his neck. When he flashed his usual, charming smile, he looked like a movie star.

Tara sidestepped past him. "Good morning."

"Good to see you back with us," he said. But his undertone held an unmistakable warning—keep quiet. He gulped back the last of his coffee, gave Kim an acknowledging nod and strode from the room.

"Is it just me, or did he seem kind of…not so happy to see you?" Kim asked.

Tara yearned to confide in her friend, but recalling Zach's warning, she shrugged off the question and poured them each a cup of coffee.

"I'll have mine black," Kim said.

Rather than risk ingesting anything from the staff fridge, Tara took hers black, too.

Zach popped his head in the door. "Hey, everything okay?"

His warm smile chased away the chill Whittaker had left in his wake. Kim's surprised gaze ping-ponged from Zach to Tara, and settled back on Zach with a recognition that made Tara's heart plummet.

If Kim knew he was a cop, she could blow his cover.

"I was wondering when I'd—?" Kim started to say, but stopped abruptly when Zach's fellow IT consultant appeared at the door.

Zach flashed Kim an almost imperceptible signal of appreciation.

Oh, yeah, they knew each other.

"You working or not?" Barb, the IT specialist griped, sounding only half teasing.

"I'll be right there. Just grabbing a coffee." Zach reached for the pot and whispered to Tara, "Let's have lunch."

She glanced from Kim to the now-empty doorway and lowered her voice to a matching whisper. "Are you sure you want to be seen with me? Might make the killer suspicious of you."

Zach gave her a quirky grin and shook his head.

"I'm just a lonely IT consultant hitting on the best-looking nurse in the hospital."

Her stomach did a little flip. Since Zach had come to town, it had been getting a steady workout. He was just watching out for her, she reminded herself.

He gave her hand a gentle tap. "I'll see you later." As he left, he winked at Kim.

The instant he was gone, Kim's attention swung to Tara. "How well do you know Zach?"

"Uh…" Tara sipped her coffee to give her stalled brain a second to figure out what to say. What if she was wrong about Kim knowing Zach was a cop? She couldn't risk blowing his cover. "I just met him last week. Why?"

Kim buffed an invisible spot on the counter.

Tara waited silently, pretty sure she wouldn't want to hear whatever Kim had to say. And not sure why.

"It's just that the two of you seem to be hitting it off," she finally said in an awkward falsetto.

"Is that a problem?"

"I'm sorry, that didn't come out right." She tugged at her ponytail, studied her shoes. "I'm not quite sure how to say this, but I feel like I should warn you. About Zach."

As Zach finished testing Dr. Whittaker's office computer, he caught sight of Kim leading a young man in shackles out of the building. Good thing Rick had had the foresight to advise her that Zach was in town undercover. One potential disaster averted.

He hoped he hadn't left another one behind him. Kim had seemed fine when he'd broken things off with her last year after a few dates, but…

Maybe he was better off not thinking what the two women might be discussing now.

Zach pulled his pass card from the computer hub and rose to see if Tara was ready to go for lunch.

His phone on his hip caught the edge of the desk blotter. As he straightened the blotter, he noticed the corner of a note page that had been tucked inside. It was a list of names, and Ellen Clark—their most recent alleged victim—was one of them. He didn't recognize any of the other names, but his gut told him this was big. Really big.

He jotted the names into his notepad. His cell phone vibrated.

Glancing at the closed door, he picked up.

"I've got an answer for you on Tara's ex," Rick said. "His neighbor confirmed that Peterson's been out of work for a few months. He does a lot of buying and selling on eBay."

"Makes you wonder where he gets the stuff he's selling."

"Last night I found baseball cards up for auction. So the story he gave Tara seems to check out."

"And his prints don't match the one on the lunch container?"

"Nope. You really didn't think he was connected to the case, did you?"

"No, but I still don't like it. If he's that desperate for money, what else might he come after?"

"The best we can do is advise her to be careful."

Yeah. Except that wasn't good enough. Not by a long shot. Jerk ex-husbands knew their wives well enough to get around their defenses. Look how easily Earl had convinced Tara to let him inside the house.

Zach pocketed his phone and headed to the nurse's station.

Tara stood divvying meds into tiny plastic cups. She leaned forward, and her thick chestnut hair fell over her eyes.

Something went warm and soft inside him. He remembered how he used to tease his wife about her hair doing that. He didn't want to remember how she'd smile back, knowing he'd tuck the wayward locks behind her ear and steal a kiss. But he did remember. Then he thought of the kiss he'd stolen from Tara in the playground.

Her gaze lifted, those big, doe-brown eyes, so like Carole's, smiling up at him.

Reflexively, his hand reached for her hair. She tensed, and his good senses kicked in. He snapped his hand back to his side.

"I'll be another twenty minutes," she said. "Why don't I meet you in the cafeteria?"

"Right." He forced his feet to move, but sideswiped by a sudden wave of guilt, it took a few seconds longer to get his thoughts back in gear. Apparently he wasn't any more ready to move on than he had been a year ago.

With too little time to start in on the next computer and his fellow consultant nowhere in sight, Zach decided to pay the beleaguered young couple he'd met a few days ago another visit. When he'd stopped by yesterday, Melanie had been much more optimistic about her prognosis, and surprisingly reticent about discussing the alternative-treatment options she'd been exploring. He hoped that meant she didn't intend to push Jeff away.

As Zach approached Melanie's room, the sound of heated voices drifted through the partially closed door.

"Her temp is a hundred and five, doctor. We need to give her something."

"No," Melanie protested weakly.

Zach edged closer and could see Alice Bradshaw wiping the girl's perspiring face with a wet cloth.

McCrae reached for Melanie's wrist and checked her pulse. "If the temp continues to climb, or doesn't come down within half an hour, page me."

"Yes, Doctor," Nurse Bradshaw grumbled.

As McCrae exited, Zach turned away from the door and feigned interest in a poster on the wall. He wavered outside the room. In Melanie's present condition, she wouldn't want a visitor.

Her fiancé stepped off the elevator with a lilt in his step.

Zach's heart went out to him. He knew all too well the roller-coaster emotions of watching a loved one battle cancer. "Hey, you're looking cheerier these days. Melanie agree to the wedding?"

A grin split Jeff's face. "Yup."

"That's great news." Zach gave him a congratulatory handshake. "Still planning to head to Mexico?"

"No. We agreed staying here is better."

"Have you decided on a particular clinic?"

From inside the room, Melanie moaned.

"Uh…" Jeff threw a worried glance past Zach. "Excuse me. I need to go to her."

Nurse Bradshaw brushed past Zach, muttering something about pigheaded patients and spineless doctors.

His curiosity piqued, Zach caught up with her. "Is it common to let a fever rage without giving a patient something to combat it?"

She scowled. "Not in my thirty years of practice."

"Yeah, didn't a patient die a couple of weeks ago from seizures brought on by a high fever?"

Bradshaw stopped walking and looked at him suspiciously. "Are you a relative?"

"No, just curious."

"Well, we're not allowed to discuss patient care. If you'll excuse me." She disappeared into the next patient's room.

Very curious.

Zach headed to the cafeteria, reminding himself to stay focused on the case.

Tara waved to him from the back corner. A plate of food sat on the table in front of her.

He glanced at the long line of people waiting for a hot meal and opted for a prepackaged sandwich and juice. Forgoing a tray, he jumped the queue, paid for his lunch and wound through the maze of tables. Between scraping chairs, the clatter of dishes and the hum of voices, he wouldn't have to worry about being overheard. He took the seat opposite Tara at the small, round table. "You look tired."

"Hmm, thanks. Just what a woman likes to hear." She dug into her liver and onions—today's special.

Zach stifled a shudder. Only medical professionals could convince themselves that something so unappetizing was good for them. "Sorry, I didn't mean to—"

"It's okay. I *am* tired." She glanced at him for only an instant and then seemed to pay an inordinate amount of attention to her food. "Suzie spiked a fever after you left yesterday. I was up most of the night."

"Is she okay?" Zach barely resisted the urge to reach out to her.

"She's home with my mom today. But she's already improving."

To keep his hands occupied, he unwrapped his sandwich. "Did you give her something to bring down her fever?"

"Of course. High fevers can be dangerous."

"Then why would a patient refuse medication?"

Tara's fork stopped midair. "He wouldn't."

"Melanie just did. Adamantly."

Lowering her fork, Tara let out a sigh, and with it, the last of her energy seemed to drain from her body. "Melanie's terminal. I guess she's decided to stop fighting."

"No, I don't think so. She's planning to marry."

"Really?" Tara frowned. "Then her refusal is strange." Her gaze strayed to a nearby table, or rather to Dr. McCrae, who was preoccupied with testing his blood sugar. "The fever might've made Melanie delirious," she speculated, her attention flitting briefly back to Zach, before returning to her food.

Her unease gnawed at his conscience. He touched her hand. "Are you mad at me?"

She looked surprised by the question, but he didn't miss the way she slipped her hand beneath the table. Maybe his quip about hitting on the prettiest nurse had her worried.

"No, of course I'm not mad. Not at all. I'm just… distracted. I'll check on Melanie as soon as I've finished lunch." She took another bite of liver.

Zach pushed aside his sandwich, strangely unsettled by her denial. Something had changed. She was even tenser now than when she'd found her ex-husband on her doorstep. "Has your ex tried to contact you again?"

Humor sparkled in her eyes. "You mean since you called me at eleven last night to ask the same question?"

Relieved to hear the teasing note in her voice, he quirked an unapologetic smile. "Do you mind?"

"No, it's nice that you care." A faint blush colored her cheeks. "And, no, I haven't heard from him, or seen him, but…my spare key is missing."

"What? From where?"

"I kept it under a rock by my door. As I left this morning, I thought I should grab it. You know, just in case. Only, it wasn't there."

"When's the last time you saw it?"

"That's just it.… I can't remember. It's just for emergencies, and I rarely use it. I may have just forgotten to put it back. I didn't have time to go inside and check around."

"That settles it. I'm changing your locks. I'll pick up the stuff I need after work and then come straight over."

"That's not necessary," she protested. "I'm sure I can figure out how to change a dead bolt."

"I don't doubt it, but it's no trouble."

For a moment, she looked as though she might argue, but then simply nodded. She had too much determination for her own good. He would've liked nothing more than to spirit her out of town until this case was resolved, but the truth was he needed her eyes and ears here.

"Has anyone behaved suspiciously around you this morning?"

"I still don't trust Whittaker," she admitted.

Yeah, he was beginning to agree. Zach pulled out his notepad with the list of names he'd found on Whittaker's desk and slid the pad across the table. "Do these names mean anything to you?"

Tara scanned the list and put her finger on the third name from the bottom. "Ellen's the woman who died last week. The others are also cancer patients." She bit her lip. "I'm not supposed to tell you that. Why do you want to know? Who are they?"

Unwilling to ask her to breach her patients' privacy further, Zach tucked the notepad back into his pocket. "I'm not sure, yet." Unfortunately, accessing the patient records was not only illegal, it could jeopardize a possible prosecution if it came out at trial. Not to mention he probably couldn't decipher them anyway.

"Where'd you get those names?"

"That's not important." Knowing they came from Whittaker's office would only fuel her curiosity. "I just wondered if there was a common link between them. Sounds like it's that they're all cancer patients." And with Ellen already dead, one of the others could be next.

A buzz sounded from Tara's purse. She dug out her phone and paled the instant she looked at the screen. Her gaze dodged around the room.

Zach pried the phone from her clenched fingers. The sender's name and number were blocked, but from Tara's reaction the text message—*Feeling better?*— was no friendly inquiry.

He could almost hear the taunting, saccharine tone.

Whittaker entered the cafeteria and beelined to their table. "Miss Peterson, there was an urgent call for you at the nurse's station. Something about your daughter."

SEVEN

Tara jerked to her feet. *Please, God, no. Not my daughter.* She was halfway out of the cafeteria before Zach's voice registered.

He pushed his cell phone into her hand. "I dialed your home number."

She clutched the phone to her ear. The machine clicked on. "Mom, pick up. What's going on? Mom, are you there?"

Zach took back the phone. "Come on, I'll drive you home."

Tara spotted Alice heading into the cafeteria and flagged her. "I have to leave. Family emergency."

"So you got the message?"

"What message?"

"Your sister Susan wanted you to call her."

Tara whipped out her phone and clicked Susan's name. Why would her sister call about Suzie? As the phone rang unanswered, unimaginable possibilities twisted her stomach.

On the fourth ring, Susan finally picked up.

"Susan, what's going on? Where's Suzie?"

"With me. Mom didn't feel well and asked me to take her. I called so you wouldn't worry."

"She's with you now? She's okay? No one…?" Tara let the question trail off, not wanting to voice her fears now that she knew her little girl was safe.

"She's fine."

Tara's shoulders sagged with relief. "Thanks. I owe you one."

"Don't sweat it. I love having my little namesake for a visit. Why don't you enjoy a nap after work? I'll give Suzie supper and bring her by later. I'm sure you didn't get a wink last night from worrying about her."

Tara groaned. Her sister knew her far too well. Whenever Suzie got a fever, Tara feared the worst. Came from caring for the terminally ill, day in and day out, she supposed. "Thanks, I might do that." She clicked off and turned to Zach. "False alarm."

"Not quite."

"What do you mean?"

"The text message." He escorted her onto the elevator and then asked to borrow her phone. "I'll see if Rick can trace the call."

Oh, right. She pressed the button for the fourth floor. She probably would've spent the rest of the day fretting about the caller's motive and next move, except the elevator doors swished opened to the blare of a code-blue alarm.

Dr. McCrae emerged from the stairwell and blazed past them.

Tara grabbed a crash cart and dashed after him, only then realizing that the alarm was for Mrs. Wainwright.

McCrae had started CPR by the time Tara wheeled in the cart.

"The patient has a Do Not Resuscitate order," Tara said.

A candy striper, who must've pulled the alarm, stood with her back pressed to the wall. The two staff members rushing in behind Tara ground to a halt. One pulled the curtain around the patient in the neighboring bed.

Tara turned Mrs. Wainwright's wristband and pointed to the DNR notation.

Grimacing, McCrae withdrew his hands and put his stethoscope to the woman's chest. He glanced at his watch. "Time of death, one thirty-two."

The other staff backed out of the room as Tara noted the time. She turned off the monitors and alarm, and set about removing the tubes and wires.

McCrae stood at the end of the bed, his fingers clenched around the rail. Whether from frustration or irritation, Tara wasn't sure.

Death affected each staff member differently. She usually coped by going for a grueling run. After failing to save Mrs. Parker a couple of weeks ago, Tara had found McCrae hunched over in the staff lounge with his head in his hands. "Mrs. Wainwright lived a good, long life." Tara tucked the blanket under the woman's chin. "She was ready to go."

"Do you really believe that? Because I don't understand how people can give up fighting."

Tara eased the IV from beneath her patient's papery skin. The scent of rose-milk hand lotion transported her back to her grandmother's house and childhood tea parties with Gran. She blinked back tears. "They aren't giving up so much as hoping for something better."

"So you believe in life after death?"

She shrugged. She taught Suzie about God and heaven, but as much as she wanted to, she didn't quite share her daughter's childlike faith. Surely if God really cared, He would have stopped Earl from leaving Suzie fatherless. "I'd like to think that there's a heaven."

He let out a heavy sigh and turned toward the door. "I suppose we all do."

"Oh, could you check on Melanie Rivers as you go? I'm concerned about her fever."

"The girl's fine. I was just in to see her," he said, in the abrasive tone residents reserved for nurses who questioned their judgment.

"Glad to hear it." Tara straightened her shoulders. "Because after what happened to Mrs. Parker, we can't be too careful."

"The two cases are nothing alike. And as I recall, you didn't think the fever killed that poor woman."

Remembering Zach's warning not to talk about her suspicions, Tara swallowed her response.

"What do you suppose the person you saw in her room was doing?"

She chewed her bottom lip. "I don't know."

"No theories?"

Her gaze skittered to his hospital-issued lab coat. "No."

Dr. McCrae looped his stethoscope around his neck. "Probably some kid trying to pinch a few pills for a cheap thrill. The hospital I interned at had a couple of guys who would pose as visitors and go room to room looking for meds the patients hadn't taken. I mentioned it to our security, so they'd keep a closer watch on the cameras."

"Yes, that would explain it." *Very well.* If Mr. Parker had caught a thief in the act, the kid would've naturally panicked and knocked him down to try and get away. Except a panicked kid wouldn't come back and poison her lunch or send her creepy text messages. Although...he might shoot at her from a passing car. She stifled a sudden shiver. No, Zach had said the car shooting wasn't related.

Tara finished tending to Mrs. Wainwright, then ushered in the grieving family.

With a heavy heart, she returned to the nurse's station, where she pulled out the trays of afternoon meds she'd prepared. She consulted the med list and removed Mrs. Wainwright's cup from the tray. But when she opened the cabinet to return the pills, the oxycodone bottle was missing. She rearranged the rows. The bottle had to be there.

But it wasn't.

"I heard your patient died," Zach said from behind her.

She jerked around, flustered that she hadn't heard his approach. He could've been anyone.

He steadied her arm. "You okay?"

She ignored the way her heart fluttered at his gentle question and even gentler touch, and took a step back. "Yes, thank you." Thank goodness Kim had warned her that his effect on women was utterly unintentional.

To be honest, she'd been relieved to hear it, and yet sadly disappointed.

"Is there anything I should know?" he asked.

Tara blinked, taking a second to realize he was asking if she suspected foul play in Mrs. Wainwright's death. "No, the patient was in her nineties, wanted to go."

"McCrae seemed unusually uptight for that to be the case."

"DNRs get to him. He can't comprehend how people can give up on living."

Zach's head tilted and he searched her eyes. "Do you see them as giving up? That there's nothing for us after death?"

"Patients get tired of fighting." She fiddled with the cup of pills. "I can understand that. Most hope something better is waiting for them."

"You sound skeptical—about the *something better,* I mean."

"I suppose I am. A little."

The admission made Zach's eyes dim, and suddenly she wasn't as troubled by the missing pain meds as much as the notion that she'd disappointed him somehow.

"Mr. Reynolds?"

Zach glanced at the outpatient clinic's receptionist, unsure how long she'd been trying to get his attention. He'd been too preoccupied rehashing his conversation with Tara for the use of his alias to register.

He closed the printer door. "Yeah, go ahead."

The printer whirred into action.

His thoughts returned to Tara. From the Bible picture books he'd noticed in her house, and the fact that she prayed with Suzie before bed, he'd assumed she was a believer. His wife's hope in an eternity with her Savior had, at times, been the only thing that held him together after her death. He'd drawn closer to God, and naturally assumed that Tara would have done the same after her husband's abandonment

To make matters worse, she stirred feelings in him that he'd thought he would never experience again, feelings he wouldn't be free to act on if she didn't share his faith.

Right. She was his informant. Or at least, that's how the prosecutor would see her. For that reason alone, he should keep his feelings to himself.

What was he saying?

He stroked the place once occupied by his wedding band. He was attracted to Tara, sure. But he could never feel for another woman what he'd shared with Carole. They'd had a once-in-a-lifetime kind of love. He kneaded the bunched muscles in the back of his neck, and looked around the room.

Two couples remained in the waiting area. An elderly couple sat near the desk, bathed in the orange glow of the late-afternoon sun shining through the glass ceiling. The woman was on oxygen, yet she serenely knitted away at a tiny sweater. A middle-aged couple, the man shivering and pale, sat huddled in the corner, draped in shadows.

A nurse entered the waiting area from the hall beyond. "Peter Campbell, this way, please."

Zach's interest was piqued. Peter Campbell was one of the names on the list he'd found in Whittaker's office. The hunched man followed the nurse down the hall to an examining room. Whittaker slipped into a small room next to the reception area as the previous patient exited.

"Is that another office?" Zach asked the clerk.

"Yes, after seeing each patient, the doctor goes there to dictate his report."

A few minutes later, Whittaker headed to the room where Peter Campbell waited.

"I'll just check out that system while Whittaker's in with the patient," Zach said, then slipped into the office. If he had the printer half-apart when Whittaker came back, the doc might ignore his presence as readily as he would a janitor or a copier repairman.

The clerk tapped on the door and opened it without waiting for a response. "Dr. Whittaker wants to see a CT-scan report, but I don't know how to upload it to the patient's medical record with this new software. Can you help?"

"No problem." Zach followed her back to the reception desk and clicked the tab that brought up the list of the day's reports. Three were from radiology. Zach showed the clerk how to open the first report and check the name and ID number.

"That's not it. I'm looking for Mr. Campbell's." She opened the second report. "This is the one."

Zach skimmed the incomprehensible shorthand, which only confirmed his supposition that even if he peeked at the patient's medical records, he'd have a hard time making sense of them. Before he could glean any useful information from the report, the clerk pressed him for help appending it to Campbell's records. Unfortunately, that process didn't afford him a glimpse of the record, either. Zach scanned the remaining list of reports and debated whether to hover over the clerk long enough to see if any of them were for other patients on Whittaker's list.

The nurse retrieved the last patient from the waiting room, and Zach decided he didn't have time. "If you've got the hang of this," he said to the clerk, "I'll finish with the other office."

When Dr. Whittaker opened the door a few minutes

later, Zach busied himself shaking and reinserting the toner and then fiddling with the paper trays. "Sorry, sir, I won't be long."

"Take your time." Whittaker sat at the computer desk and inserted his card into the hub. Campbell's CT-scan report appeared on the screen. "This is unbelievable."

Zach held his breath, waiting, hoping Whittaker would explain.

"The tumor shrank three centimeters in four weeks," Whittaker muttered to himself. "Without treatment. Could this be some sort of delayed effect?"

Campbell was getting better? *Interesting.*

"Reynolds, is there a way for me to add notes to this report?"

Zach put down his cleaning brush. "Certainly, sir." He took over the mouse and demonstrated how to open a text box to add comments. "When you're done, you click here to save and close."

As Zach returned his attention to the printer, Whittaker typed in his comments. Then, without so much as a glance at Zach, he clicked on the Dictaphone and rattled off his report on the patient's visit. "After seeing no reduction in tumor growth, Peter Campbell withdrew from the AP-2000 trials eight weeks ago, yet his condition has now improved."

Zach's hands stilled at the mention of drug trials. Was this the connection among the patients on Whittaker's list?

"If this trend continues," Whittaker rambled on,

"Campbell's prognosis looks promising. He continues to take oxycodone for pain. Follow up in a month." Whittaker clicked off the microphone, pulled his card from the computer hub and exited the room.

Oxycodone. Tara had mentioned Whittaker's unusual interest in the pain med. And what was AP-2000?

Zach quickly reassembled the printer and hurried back to Tara's ward. He ran into Jeff at the elevator. "Hey, how's Melanie doing?"

"Good. The doctor might release her tomorrow." Jeff's positive spin sounded forced.

"After the fever she had today?"

"You heard about that?"

Zach smirked. "From the way Nurse Bradshaw griped about Melanie's refusal to take anything for it, I'm sure everyone on the floor heard about it."

Jeff groaned.

"Why didn't she want to take anything?"

"I don't know." Jeff toed the baseboard. "She's been poked and prodded for so long, she's been itching for a fight."

That was better than giving up as Tara had supposed. For Jeff's sake, Zach hoped she was wrong. But the shuttered look in the other man's eyes suggested that perhaps he feared the same.

By the time Zach reached the nurse's station, Tara had clocked out. Through the window at the stairwell, he caught sight of Barb, his fellow IT consultant, and Dr. Whittaker walking arm in arm to Whittaker's red

Maserati. Terrific. The one woman expert enough to see through his cover was dating his prime suspect.

Zach hurried out to the parking lot and found McCrae looking under Tara's hood while she tried to start the car.

McCrae wiped his hand on a rag and went around to her window. "Sorry. Not sure what else to try. Why don't I give you a lift home and you can have your mechanic tow this to the garage?"

The offer sounded sincere, but Zach didn't like it. He jogged over to them and offered to take a look.

McCrae stepped aside.

Zach immediately spotted a loose spark plug and tightened the connection. "Try it again. No, wait." He scanned the engine, then shimmied underneath to check for evidence of tampering or explosives. Everything looked good, but to be on the safe side, he asked her to step out of the car and turned the key himself.

The engine roared to life.

"Thank you," she beamed, and then, thanking McCrae, declined his offer of a ride.

McCrae didn't seem overly disappointed.

But that didn't allay Zach's suspicions. He certainly wasn't about to let Tara head home alone to an empty house, knowing her spare key was missing.

Trouble was, before he'd reached his truck, Tara had pulled out of the parking lot. He waited a moment to see what McCrae would do. After the doc headed back inside the hospital, Zach zipped out after Tara.

Two blocks later, he got caught behind a truck with

a wide load. He cut down a side street only to hit cul-de-sac after cul-de-sac. Finally he found a street that took him back to the main road, smack behind the truck again.

He whipped out his phone and punched in Tara's number.

The phone in his pocket rang, and he cursed himself for forgetting to return it to her. He tried the house number, but the machine picked up on the first ring—which meant she was making a call. He instantly hung up in case she was trying to reach him. Spotting a hardware store, and still gridlocked behind the truck, he swerved into the parking lot to buy new dead bolts.

He was in and out in record time, but his cell phone beeped a missed message alert as he exited the store.

His heart in his throat, he snatched up the phone, then let out a breath at the sight of Rick's number. Zach returned the call.

His buddy picked up on the first ring.

"I've got a couple more comparisons for you," Zach said, referring to the fingerprints he'd collected. "I'll drop them by later."

"Use the alternate."

Alternate? The alternate was code for their backup rendezvous site. "What's wrong?"

"The pound called. The cat got out."

He'd been made? And Rick's talking in code indicated that communications might've been infiltrated. Chances were their analytics software showed increased traffic to the phony websites associated with his alias, which meant someone had checked him out.

"Okay, thanks for letting me know." If it was an analytics flag, the site traffic could be innocent. Tara might've done a search on him, or perhaps any of a number of women in the hospital who'd batted their eyes at him. But he had to assume he'd made someone nervous, or suspicious, which could mean he was close.

He pictured how cozy Whittaker and Barbara had looked. At least anyone snooping into his background would conveniently find that he used to own a computer shop. *Sort of.* It had been his cover for an operation that had cracked a major theft ring specializing in computers. And since his role in the operation never came to light, they'd left the cover in play.

But if someone had seen through it and figured out what he really was...

Tara was at greater risk than he'd feared.

EIGHT

"Forget it," Tara repeated into the phone, ready to hang up on her ex.

"Come on, Tara. You know Suzie's never going to wear that ugly broach, and you're too sentimental to sell it. So it's just going to sit in your jewelry box not doing anyone any good."

"Your mother willed that broach to Suzie. She deserves to know how special she was to her grandmother."

"So tell her. I'm desperate here. If I miss another payment, I'll lose my car."

She felt her patience dwindling. "I'm sorry about that, Earl. I truly am. But I won't let you hock Suzie's and my home out from under us so you can drive an overpriced sports car. You made your choice a long time ago."

"But—"

"Earl, I mean it. Don't call again." Tara clicked off the phone before he could utter another word. She sank onto the bed, her insides jittering. At least she didn't have to worry anymore that his sudden attempts to contact her were a ploy to gain custody of Suzie. He cared so little for his daughter that, not only hadn't he asked after her, he had no qualms about confiscating his mother's gift to her only granddaughter.

The doorbell chimed.

Interrupted by Earl's call in the middle of changing her clothes, Tara quickly pulled on a pair of jeans and T-shirt.

The doorbell chimed again.

"I'm coming," she called, stuffing the bottom of her shirt into her waistband. As she hurried through the living room, she picked up a few of the toys Suzie had left lying about.

Pounding rattled the windows. "Tara, are you okay?"

She yanked open the door. "Sorry I took so long." Tara drank in the sight of Zach on her front porch, his cheeks reddened by the cold and his jaw shadowed with early evening stubble. He hoisted a box of tools and locks from the stoop and stepped inside. His broad shoulders filled the doorway, and the mix of leather and crisp air that swirled in behind him made her breath catch.

Sure, he was handsome. But she shouldn't have noticed the intense way his honey-brown eyes searched hers.

"Are you okay?"

She finger-combed her mussed hair. "Absolutely," she lied, telling herself that Zach didn't need to know about Earl's call. Her ex was the last person she wanted to talk about. Zach was already changing the locks because of him. No reason to add more fuel to that fire and spoil the conversation.

Zach gave her a lopsided smile, and goose bumps that had nothing to do with the chill in the air rose on her arms. "Glad to hear it." He closed the door and scrutinized the dead bolt. "This shouldn't take me long to replace."

"Can I get you a soda or coffee or something first?"

"Maybe after I'm done."

He took her welfare so seriously, the complete opposite of her ex. Zach's concern went above and beyond his job description, too. She'd never heard of the police changing an attempted break-in victim's locks. Maybe Kim was wrong about him this time.... Maybe he *was* interested in her.

"Oh, and before I forget..." Zach held out her cell phone. "No luck tracing the call, I'm afraid."

She pressed her palms to her sides. "Maybe you should keep that in case he leaves another message."

Zach's gaze brimmed with compassion. "I don't like the thought of you being without a phone in an emergency." He set it on the table. "Just leave it turned off unless you need to make a call."

She shivered at the thought of turning it on to a long list of missed messages like the weird one she'd gotten at lunchtime. She fisted her hands, angry that some maniac had forced this chaos into her life. She was tired of looking over her shoulder. There had to be more they could do to catch this guy.

Tara proposed Dr. McCrae's theft theory to Zach.

"If the guy in Mrs. Parker's room had been trying to steal her medication and Mr. Parker surprised him, the thief might have pushed him in a panic to escape. It explains Mr. Parker's head injury."

"Doesn't explain his wife's death. Or Ellen's. She wasn't at the hospital when she started seizing."

Tara blew out an exasperated breath. "Maybe *I'm* wrong about the patient deaths. Maybe the guy targeted me because I caught him in the room and he's afraid he'll be charged for Mr. Parker's death."

"Mr. Parker told you the person killed his wife. That's why I'm on this case."

"Maybe Mrs. Parker saw the guy take her medication and he killed her to keep her quiet."

"She had no sign of trauma on her body."

Tara pressed her palm to her pounding head. "It's a hospital. He could've injected her with one of a half dozen different drugs that would kill her and go undetected. Anything from potassium to insulin."

"But if he had access to those kind of drugs, why would he steal from patients' rooms?"

Possible scenarios had been swirling through her mind at such a dizzying rate she couldn't think straight anymore. She ran her fingers through her hair. "I don't know. It was just a theory."

"I'm not knocking it. Honest. This is how investigations play out. We entertain different theories and work them through to see if they match what we know."

"What I know is that a bottle of oxycodone went missing this afternoon. Lots of cancer patients are on similar pain pills. Pain pills that score a lot of money on the street. The theory may not explain the fevers, but it's more than you've come up with." She cupped her hand over her mouth, then lowered it sheepishly. "I'm sorry. I didn't mean that the way it sounded."

"No apology necessary." His gentle voice soothed her ragged nerves. "Investigations are rarely as straightforward as we'd like." He looked as though he might say more, but then hefted his toolbox and headed for the back door. "Okay. If someone's skimming drugs, he's probably selling them on the street. It's a good angle. I'll ask Rick to press his street informants for information."

She trailed after him. "No, that doesn't make sense. A doctor could simply sell a prescription to a dealer and claim his pad was stolen. He wouldn't risk getting caught pilfering a pill here and there."

"Whoever shoved you isn't necessarily a doctor. He could've worn a lab coat so patients wouldn't question why he was in their room."

The doorbell chimed. She glanced out the front window. "That's my sister bringing Suzie home."

The moment Tara opened the door, Suzie peered past Tara's legs. "Where Dak?"

Zach stepped around the corner of the kitchen, and Suzie bolted straight to him. "Dak back," she squealed, lifting her hands.

Zach scooped her into a bear hug and was rewarded with a bellyful of giggles.

"Ahh," Susan said, "you must be the doc Suzie's

been chattering about all day. She went nuts when she saw your truck in the driveway."

He set Suzie down and extended his hand to Tara's sister. "Zach. Pleased to meet you."

"He's a computer consultant, not a doctor," Tara clarified.

Suzie recaptured Zach's attention, and Susan sent Tara a telling smile. "Ni-i-ice."

"Will you stay for coffee?" Tara spun toward the kitchen before her sister noticed the blush heating her cheeks. It had to be Earl's total disregard for Suzie that made Zach's adoration seem so absolute.

To Tara's relief, Susan tactfully declined the coffee offer.

Suzie scurried to her room and came running back with her teddy, her blankie and a bedtime story. "Read dis one to me." She stretched up her arm, bobbing the book in front of Zach, her eyes glowing with anticipation.

Tara's heart did a slow roll in her chest. He was so good for her daughter. But Suzie was getting *too* attached. Tara didn't want Suzie's tender heart broken when this case ended and Zach left. Soon enough, she'd face taunts from school kids over being abandoned by her father. She didn't need a trail of father figures doing the same.

Zach glanced up from the Bible story he was reading to Suzie. Tara sat at the opposite end of the sofa, her gaze considerably cooler than it had been a few minutes ago. Was she mad at him for indulging Suzie's request? Or was it the story that left her cold?

The sense that she might not share his faith bothered him more than he wanted to admit.

By the time he reached the end of the story, Suzie was sound asleep, snuggled against his chest, thumb in her mouth, blanket and teddy crunched under her arm. The picture of contentment. *Oh, Lord, I could get used to this in a hurry.*

"Shall I carry her to bed?" he whispered to Tara.

Tara's head bobbed as if she'd been jolted out of a daydream. "Yes, thank you." She rose and led the way down the hall.

After a week of seeing Tara's big brown eyes every day and working around cancer patients, he thought he'd gotten his volatile feelings under control. But the sight of Suzie's room, decorated in soft pinks and frilly lace, sucker punched him.

His wife had begun decorating their spare room about thirty seconds after her pregnancy was confirmed. The cancer diagnosis had come two months later, but she'd continued to pour her heart into that room.

A wave of grief and loss swept through him.

Laying Suzie gently on the bed, he struggled to recover his composure.

Tara tucked a comforter around her sleeping child and gently kissed her on the forehead. "Sweet dreams, honey."

Watching Tara with Suzie heightened the yearning

he didn't want to feel. He couldn't explain how the pair had so quickly dug their way through the wall he'd built around his heart, but they had.

He returned to the door lock he'd been working on when Suzie had arrived.

Tara filled the kettle with water. "Tea okay?"

"Great, thanks." Zach debated how to broach the subject on his mind. His feelings were already more entangled than they should be. He fitted the new lock into place and tightened the screws. "Suzie's a sweet girl. You've done a terrific job raising her."

Tara's face lit up. "Thank you. A mother doesn't hear that too often."

"She seems to really like the Bible stories. Does she go to Sunday school?"

"Yes, she adores it."

"And you?"

"Me?" She averted her eyes.

"Earlier today you didn't seem convinced that there's something to look forward to after death."

"Oh." She hesitated. "I want to," she said with a hint of reluctance. "It's just that working at the hospital… It's hard, you know? I admit that I've seen some miraculous recoveries, but I see a lot of patients whose prayers aren't answered, too."

Zach returned his tools to his toolbox and joined her at the kitchen table. "That doesn't make God any less real. Sometimes his answer is no."

"I'm sorry." Tara's voice turned soft. "Kim told me about your wife."

His heart pitched. Was that why she'd hedged his question? She didn't want to hurt him by admitting her doubts.

The pity on Tara's face reminded him why he'd never told Rick or any of his colleagues about his former life. He'd only told Kim so she wouldn't blame herself for the way things had worked out between them.

"Just as you have reasons for not giving Suzie everything she asks for, I have to believe that God knew what was best." He rubbed the hollow at the base of his ring finger and cleared his throat. "My wife slipped away peacefully, with the certainty that she was a breath away from heaven. If not for that, I think I would've gone crazy with grief."

"So you're a believer? Even though God took your wife?"

His eyes slipped shut. "My wife. And…" He swallowed, but the grief remained firmly balled in his throat. "And," he repeated, his voice hoarse, "our stillborn child."

Tara's warm hand covered his, and a funny catch hiccupped in his chest. "I'm so sorry."

Shoring up his defenses, he drew in a deep breath. "My wife made me promise her that I wouldn't blame God."

Tara nodded, withdrew her hand and busied herself pouring tea. "I don't think I could've kept that promise. I've seen God let too many people down."

"Trusting in God doesn't mean you won't face troubles. I think my wife understood that better than me. If not for my promise to her, I probably would've let my grief turn to anger at God."

Tara gave him a wry smile. "Yeah, been there."

"For the longest time, I clung to my faith out of sheer determination to keep my promise," Zach admitted. "Getting angry would've been a whole lot easier, because, yeah, I felt like He let us down. And I got pretty tired of hearing people spout the usual platitudes."

"So, what changed?"

His mind drifted back to his first week as a cop. "I had to deliver a baby. It was a wet, miserable day. Rush hour. No time to transport, and the cord wrapped around the baby's neck." Sudden tears blurred Zach's vision at the recollection. "There I was on a busy street, holding this precious life in my hands, the same way I'd held my own baby girl the year before."

Tara's hand flew to her mouth and her big, brown eyes grew watery, too.

Zach smiled. "Only this child was bawling at the indignity of being brought into the world in the backseat of her dad's beat-up Chevy. By the time I handed the infant over to an ambulance attendant, my entire body was shaking. The baby's father threw his arms around me and said thank-you, over and over."

Zach pressed his fingers to his eyes and swallowed hard. "He said, 'I prayed for a miracle and God sent you.' *Me.* I was his miracle. In that instant, the sun beamed through the clouds as if God was saying, 'I know you're hurting, but I still have work for you here.'"

Tara leaned back against the counter, staring at him mutely, her tea apparently forgotten.

He waited, not knowing what to say, worried he'd already said too much. He'd wanted to convince her she could trust God, not fuel her doubts. When she didn't say anything either, he rose. "It's getting late. I should get going."

"Oh." She shook her head as if her mind had been elsewhere.

Thinking about God, he hoped. "By the way, when did Kim tell you about my wife?"

"After you invited me to lunch." Tara's lips twitched at the corners. "She was afraid I might be falling for you."

"Really?" He gave her a lopsided grin. "Are you?"

She matched his grin with a teasing one of her own, and a warm zing shot through his chest. "Don't worry. I'm no more interested in starting something than she says you are."

Zach let his gaze drop to Tara's lips. *Oh, Kim has no idea.* "In my line of work, you learn not to believe everything you're told."

NINE

Tara shouldn't have been surprised when her sister showed up at the house at five-thirty the next morning...just in case Suzie's fever had returned, barring her return to daycare. As soon as Tara accepted the offer to babysit, Susan leaned back on the sofa, her eyes sparkling with curiosity. "So-o-o, tell me about your new guy."

Tara spread her uniform over the ironing board and swiped at it with the iron. "He's not my 'new' guy."

Susan pitched forward. "He's not new? How long have you been holding out on me?"

Tara rolled her eyes. "He's not my guy at all."

"Trust me. Any guy who volunteers to change your locks—on hockey night, no less—is totally *gaga* over you. Did you not see how adorable he was with Suzie?"

Suzie looked up from her cereal bowl.

"It's okay, honey," Tara said. "You can keep eating." To her sister, Tara shot a cool-it-or-else glare and lowered her voice. "I will not put Suzie through another Earl."

"You can't go through the rest of your life trying to protect yourself from worst-case scenarios. You'll never find another guy."

"I don't need another guy to be happy." She snatched up her uniform and slipped into the bathroom to dress.

"You may not need one," Susan called out from the living room. "But that guy makes you happy. You were practically glowing last night."

Tara glanced at the mirror, confirming the rush of color Susan's comment had brought to her cheeks. She had to admit that, since listening to Zach talk so openly about his wife and daughter, it was getting harder to convince herself that he'd wind up hurting her the way Earl had. And surely anyone with a faith that had weathered as many trials as his wouldn't walk away from a covenant made before God.

What was she thinking?

Zach wasn't interested in marrying her. Or *anyone,* if Kim could be believed. Except…

Tara's heart fluttered at the memory of Zach's parting words not to believe everything she was told. Banishing the whimsical daydream, she rejoined her sister.

Susan hugged her knees to her chest and lowered her voice to a whisper. "Has he kissed you yet?"

Tara nibbled on her bottom lip.

"He *did.* All right, sis!"

"It was just a silly game he was playing with Suzie. It didn't mean anything." If it had, he would've tried again by now. Wouldn't he…?

His parting words whispered through her mind yet again, and she had to rein in the smile that tugged at her lips.

"Methinks she protests too much."

She shot her sister a warning look. "Susan, I mean it. Stop."

"You've got to get Earl's voice out of your head. You're not that hard to live with. And I should know. I shared a bedroom with you for sixteen years."

"I appreciate the vote of confidence, but I like my life the way it is."

"Routine, predictable, boring." Susan counted off on her fingers.

"Exactly." Tara lifted Suzie down from the chair and set the dirty dishes in the sink.

"Come on. So you're a little organizationally challenged and can't balance a checkbook to save your life—you've got lots of great qualities guys love."

"Sure, whatever you say." Tara grabbed her purse and gave Suzie a big kiss goodbye.

"You do. You're smart. You're creative. You have more energy than anyone I know. And you whip up delicious five-course meals for our family get-togethers without breaking a sweat." Susan gazed cajolingly at her. "Come on. Live a little. What happened to my spontaneous big sister who was always up for an adventure?"

"She became a mother. I can't have men coming into Suzie's life, building false hopes that they'll stick around."

"Are you sure it's really Suzie you're trying to protect?" Susan asked.

"I've got to run. Thanks so much for staying with Suzie."

Two hours later, Dr. Whittaker summoned Tara from his office doorway.

Tara held up a finger to signal him to give her a minute and finished ushering her patient to his room. By the time she turned back to Whittaker, he was storming toward her.

"Is there a problem?"

"A big one." He cupped her elbow and steered her in the direction of his office.

Her thoughts flew to the meds that had gone missing yesterday. Except, how would he know? And he wasn't her boss anyway. Which meant...

She glanced in the direction she'd last spotted Zach, but he was nowhere in sight. No one was. Her thoughts spiraled through a half-dozen potential problems Whittaker might wish to *discuss,* even as a tiny voice in the back of her mind said, *Run.*

Whittaker motioned her to precede him into his office and, despite the added privacy, lowered his voice. "The lab results came in from Ellen Clark's autopsy."

Tara blinked. Ellen's autopsy was the last thing she'd thought Whittaker would want to discuss. "What did they find?"

"High concentrations of bacteria at the site of her IV shunt."

"Contamination?" she gasped.

"Looks that way. I want all patients checked for signs of infection, and extra precautions taken when administering IVs to guard against further incidents."

"I can assure you, my nurses take every precaution to—"

"You can assure me all you want, but if this goes to a lawsuit, who do you think they'll blame?"

As much as Zach wanted to squirrel himself away in a private office and investigate the names on Whittaker's list, he divided his time between helping irritated staff members figure out how to navigate the new computer software, and documenting the bugs they uncovered. The work was mind-numbingly tedious, because first he had to figure out whether the user was just doing something wonky, such as hitting the enter key fifty times in two seconds in impatience. But if Barb was the person checking out his cover story, he couldn't afford to let the work he was "supposed" to be doing slide.

At least working side by side with a number of different staff members gave him the opportunity to soak up the hospital scuttlebutt. He heard about everything from hospital romances to complaints about mismanaged funding, and given the openness with which staff chatted, he wondered how much patients might overhear. Patients like Melanie.

She might be just the person to offer some inside information on Whittaker's drug trials.

When ten o'clock rolled around, Zach grabbed a

couple of coffees and headed to Melanie's room. Last night he'd been all set to ask Tara what she knew about the drug trials, but after hearing about the oxycodone theft and seeing how intent she was on ferreting out answers, he'd thought better of giving her more ideas that might put her at greater risk.

He tapped on Melanie's door. "Hey, there, how are you feeling today?"

The young woman sat up in bed and reached for the cup of coffee with a grin. "Better now, thanks."

"Your doctor know what caused yesterday's fever?"

Her thin shoulders lifted and fell in a dismissive shrug as she blew at the top of her steaming coffee.

Taking the hint that she didn't want to talk about her illness, he reclined in the chair next to her bed and sipped his coffee, debating how to work her around to the topic of Whittaker's drug trials. "I bet you hear all sorts of juicy stories hanging out here all day."

"You sound like my sister. She wants to know which doctors are available."

Zach grinned. "I'd settle for a pretty nurse."

As if thinking about Tara had drawn her to his side, a tap sounded at the door. "Good morning, Mel. I just need to check your IV. It'll only take a minute." Her gaze briefly met his, and a smile flitted over her lips before she walked to the opposite side of Mel's bed with a tote.

Confiding in Tara last night had left him feeling oddly uplifted.

Tara examined Melanie's arm, paying particular

attention to her IV connection, then swabbed the site with a damp cotton ball. "Looks good." She smiled, her gaze flitting to Zach's. Next she checked the IV bag, then collected the tote. "All done." Her gaze briefly met Zach's one last time before she left.

"*She's* pretty," Melanie said.

Zach's attention snapped from the doorway back to Melanie. "What?"

"I think she likes you, too."

He furrowed his forehead. "You think? How can you tell?"

"The way she kept stealing glances at you."

"Yeah, I noticed that."

"Of course…" Melanie's voice trailed off teasingly as she reached for her coffee cup. "It might've had something to do with the fact that you couldn't keep your eyes off her the entire time she was in the room."

"That obvious, huh?"

Melanie laughed. "Oh, yeah. Why don't you ask her out?"

Zach gulped the last of his coffee, hoping the heat would dissolve the sudden lump in his throat. The same lump he'd felt last night when his instincts had told him Tara was hedging his question with her "no more interested than you are" retort. A smile tugged at his lips. "You never know, I might do that."

He tossed his cup into the trash can and segued into their earlier conversation. "So with all the chitchat you've overheard, do you know anything about Tara?"

"Enough to know that she might be interested." Melanie waggled her eyebrows.

Encouraged by her relaxed mood, Zach tried to steer the discussion in the direction he needed it to go. "I got the impression she thinks highly of Dr. Whittaker." *At least until she started thinking he was a murderer.*

"Everyone loves Dr. Whittaker."

"I heard he's running trials on a new cancer drug. Has he mentioned it to you as an option?"

"He might have. I've been on so many drugs, I can't keep them straight." A frown creased her forehead. "Except to know they haven't worked."

Another dead end. Zach restrained a sigh. Maybe he'd have to quiz Tara about the trials after all. "So what's next? Have you decided on an alternative protocol?"

Melanie set her barely touched coffee cup on the bedside table and rolled onto her side. "Not really. I'm sorry.... I can't keep my eyes open. Thanks for bringing the coffee."

Zach wasn't sure what to make of the sudden dismissal. When they'd first met, she'd been excited about the prospect of trying an alternative treatment.

Exiting the room, he spotted Dr. McCrae. "Hey, Doc, can I talk to you for a minute?"

McCrae adjusted the stethoscope draped around his neck and straightened the rectangular glasses perched on his nose. "Yes?"

"A couple of days ago, Melanie talked about going

to Mexico for some special kind of treatment. Do you think it would help?"

McCrae studied him a moment. "The treatment has had promising results, but I would never recommend traveling abroad."

"She mentioned that you proposed some other options she might consider."

"I'm sorry. How are you related to Miss Rivers?"

"Just a friend," Zach said.

"Well, I'm not at liberty to discuss my patient's care with *friends*."

"No, no. I understand. I just wanted to say that I was impressed to hear a doctor offer other options. Few doctors seem to take any of the alternative therapies seriously."

"Naturally, we're concerned about potential interactions between supplements and meds." McCrae hesitated. "But personally, I think it's criminal that the only way patients can access some of the options is by traveling overseas."

"You sound pretty passionate about the alternative treatments. Like, maybe you've seen the results firsthand?"

"In a way." McCrae's gaze settled on the far wall, almost as if he was staring much farther into the distance, or into the past. A moment later, he returned his attention to Zach. "After my older brother exhausted all hope in our medical options, he traveled to Mexico for treatment."

"So the results were good?"

"No. He died."

Zach watched the doctor's face, searching for further evidence of the vacant expression he'd just witnessed, but he saw only a deep sorrow in the man's eyes. A sorrow that echoed painfully against the walls of Zach's chest.

"But that's not the point," McCrae continued. "My brother never should've felt like he had to travel thousands of miles from home for hope. And then die—" McCrae's voice cracked "—alone."

"I'm sorry. I lost my wife to cancer and can imagine how difficult that would've been for your family." Zach paused. "But if you feel that way, why would you discuss alternative-treatment options with Melanie?"

"Hope, Mr. Reynolds. It can be a miraculous healer. And the girl needs a good dose." McCrae headed into the next patient's room.

Zach stared at the open door to Melanie's room and recalled the peace on his wife's face as she'd slipped from this life.

His thoughts shifted to Tara and last night's conversation. He understood her struggle to comprehend how a loving God could allow such suffering. The Bible said that no one understands that the righteous are taken away to be spared from evil. Intellectually, he could concede that God had spared his wife and child from much worse. But deep down...

Deep down, sometimes it had taken every ounce of his will not to resent that God hadn't seen fit to spare them more.

But the alternative, doubting they'd moved on to a better place, was unthinkable. Somewhere along the way, God had filled him with an inexplicable peace, and gratefulness for the time they'd had together. If only Tara could see past her own disappointments in God.

He shook away the thought, too aware that he had other reasons for wanting Tara to believe. He needed his mind focused on the job. Not Tara. At least—not beyond her safety. He pushed the button for the elevator, contemplating a way he might quiz her about Whittaker's drug trials without raising her suspicions.

The doors opened and Tara stood inside.

"Hey, can you ride to my floor with me?" he asked.

She stepped back to let him in. "I was surprised to see you with Melanie."

A smile whispered across his lips at the memory of Melanie's take on his interest in Tara. *Focus.* He pushed the button for the third floor and waited for the elevator doors to close before responding to Tara's comment. "I'm concerned about her. I think McCrae is, too."

"But he's the one that recommended she be released tomorrow."

"Probably because he gave her the names of alternative-treatment facilities. Which I don't get. I thought this new cancer wing was supposed to be offering the most cutting-edge treatments. Why wouldn't he refer her to one of the drug trials?"

"Trust me, if McCrae thought the drugs could help

Melanie, he'd move heaven and earth to get her into one of Whittaker's trials. That's the kind of doctor he is." The elevator halted and the doors whisked open.

Zach hit the door-close button and braced his hand on the wall behind Tara's head. "What do you mean *if?*"

She lowered her voice. "Let's just say Whittaker has a tendency to get fixated on these trials. And I'm not convinced that it's always for the right reasons."

"Because drug companies pay for the tests?"

The elevator doors reopened, this time back at Tara's floor.

She slipped around him and out the doors. "You said it. Not me."

Yeah, if the drug company offered Whittaker kickbacks for good results—a kickback in the form of a hefty donation to the new cancer wing, perhaps—Whittaker might be persuaded to skew his results.

Zach found a private alcove on the next floor and put in another call to Rick. "I need you to check the coroner's reports on Ellen Clark and Debra Parker. Had either woman been on a drug called AP-2000?"

Papers rustled. "Yes. Ellen was. Not Parker. Why?"

"A theory I'm working on." Except if subjects were dying on the drugs, Whittaker would be more likely to cover up their participation in the trials than hurry along their demise. Still, something didn't add up.

"Does the theory include Alice? Because she's our fingerprint match."

TEN

Tara scanned the hall around the empty nurse's station before rounding the desk to log on to the computer. Zach may have wanted her to believe that his interest in Whittaker's drug trials was for Melanie's sake, but she didn't believe for a second that he'd let himself get sidetracked from his investigation. His interest must have to do with the list of names he'd shown her yesterday.

Zach had been pretty closed-lipped about where he'd gotten the names and why he was interested in those patients. But he'd probably appreciate any information she could feed him. Between the creepy text message and the scare over Suzie, and then the code blue yesterday, she'd completely forgotten about the list. Technically, she shouldn't look up patients' records without a valid medical reason, but what harm would a quick peek do?

She logged on to the computer and tried to recall who was on the list. Ellen was. And Chester. Yes, Chester Morton. She glanced around again to ensure no one was in the vicinity and then pulled up Chester's medical record. With a bit of digging she might be able to figure out what they all had in common.

She quickly scrolled through the files, looking for anything that seemed out of the ordinary. Chester was diagnosed with inoperable cancer four years ago. He'd endured a number of treatment protocols with limited success. Six months ago, he'd withdrawn from the AP-2000 trials. Bingo. She knew there had to be a connection between that list and Zach's sudden interest in Whittaker's drug trials.

"What's so interesting?"

Tara jerked the cursor across the screen at Alice's sudden appearance. The woman would report her in a heartbeat. Tara quickly closed Chester's file. "I was updating records. Any trouble while I was gone?"

"Chelsea's sister is here again. Says Chelsea needs more pain meds."

Tara opened the patient's file on the computer screen to see how long until her next dose.

"Want a coffee?" Alice poured two cups, doctored them with milk and sugar, and handed one to Tara. "You look like you could use the caffeine."

"Thanks." As Tara brought the cup to her lips and blew the liquid into tiny ripples, the phone rang. She hit Speakerphone. "May I help you?"

"Tara?" Zach said, so quietly it took her a second to recognize his voice.

She picked up the handset. "Yes."

"We have a match."

"Match?" she repeated, taking a sip of coffee.

"The fingerprint on your lunch container. It's Alice's."

She spluttered coffee across the computer screen. *Alice's?!*

"You okay?" Zach asked.

Alice had disappeared.

Tara sprinted to the sink and gargled out the remnants in her throat with a glass of water. She'd been so preoccupied with the medical records, she hadn't given Alice's coffee offer a second thought.

"Tara?" Zach's voice sounded from the handset lying on the desk.

She rinsed her mouth a couple more times, then returned to the phone. "I'm here."

"I wanted you to know so you'd be on your guard."

"Good thinking." She shuddered to think how close she'd come to downing Alice's toxic brew.

"Now, she may not be involved. She could've simply moved the container around in the fridge. But it's imperative that you act normal. Whoever poisoned your lunch seems to have taken a wait-and-see approach. I don't want you to give her, or whoever it is, a reason to come after you again."

Right. Alice had offered her the coffee after she'd caught her looking at the files.

"So far Rick hasn't been able to convince the judge we have sufficient evidence for a search warrant."

Tara wiped the coffee drips from her computer screen. "I think I can help with that."

"How do you figure?"

The bitter taste rose in Tara's throat. "She brought me a cup of coffee just before you called."

"You didn't drink any, did you?"

If she wasn't mistaken, Tara heard Zach's chair topple and imagined him surging to his feet. "I'm fine," she hedged, racking her brain for poisons potent enough to damage without being swallowed. She couldn't think of any that wouldn't have stung her throat or whose bitter taste could be covered, even by hospital coffee.

"Stay put. I'll be right there."

She spotted Alice heading toward Whittaker's office. "It'd be better if I meet you. Say, at the back door of wing C in five minutes?"

"Okay. I'll have Rick send someone over to take the cup in for testing. This could clinch our case." He paused a moment. "See you in a few minutes. Don't be late."

As she hung up the phone, Tara shivered at the thought that Alice could despise her enough to poison her.

The woman was spiteful, yes…but enough to murder her?

Tara took a deep, bolstering breath and then snatched her pass card from the computer hub. Even if Alice was behind the other attempts, she was too smart to poison a coffee that would easily be traced back to her. Tara picked up the mug. Well, they'd know soon enough. She headed for the stairwell to avoid running into anyone.

By the time she reached the back door, Zach was waiting. He took the cup with a latex-gloved hand, then caught her hand in his free one and stroked his thumb across her knuckles. "Stay alert."

He wore a denim shirt that made the blue of his eyes swirl in ever-darkening shades. Or maybe it was the way he looked at her, as if he couldn't bear to let her out of his sight.

Slipping from his grasp, she headed back upstairs. *I'm not attracted to him.* Sure, he was nice. But it had been so long since a guy had paid her any attention, she was probably reading too much into his touch, his soft words. She was his informant, for crying out loud. He couldn't care about her beyond that.

Her mind harkened back to the soul-baring story he'd shared last night about his wife. Okay, maybe he cared a little.

But *she* couldn't.

Suzie was at an impressionable age right now.

Are you sure it's really Suzie you're trying to protect?

Tara shook away the memory of her sister's probing question. Between her new position and Suzie's care, it was all she could do to maintain a steady course. She didn't need any complications. Never mind that Zach was the most incredible man she'd ever met and a natural with kids and the sweetest thing since lollipops.

I'm not attracted to him, she repeated firmly.

Zach rubbed his eyes and tried refocusing on the computer screen. He hadn't missed the way Tara's hands had trembled as she'd handed him the mug of coffee for testing. She was scared. And revealing his own anxiousness hadn't helped.

He had plenty of experience with informants in dangerous situations, but none of those situations had ever hit him like this. As though…it was personal.

Was Alice involved, or had she innocently handled Tara's lunch container? If she was guilty, there had to be other evidence he could use to nail her. As for possible motive… Was she afraid Tara had seen her in that hospital room? Or did her resentment of Tara's promotion make her a willing coconspirator with the person really behind the patients' deaths? Someone like Whittaker?

A call bell dinged, and the RN reviewing charts at the desk next to him left the station.

Taking advantage of the momentary privacy, he typed in his password and pulled up the audit records. Part of his "job" was to validate the data, but since these included a record of every time a staff member accessed the system and what files he opened, Zach was more interested in what he might discover. In the last case he'd cracked, he'd used a system audit trail to blow a suspect's alibi.

Zach opened Whittaker's records first. The man had been on and off the system from various terminals throughout the hospital. Unusual, but not unjustifiable. Zach skimmed through the list of patient medical records retrieved over the past few weeks. Most had been accessed from the stations in the outpatient clinic, but... Uh-oh, what was this?

Whittaker had accessed a dozen medical records from his office the Saturday before last. And ten of those names matched the list Zach had found. So what was he up to?

Zach scrolled forward, but there was no evidence that Whittaker had opened any of those same records in the week and a half since then. Zach tracked McCrae's trail next. His access to medical records was far more sporadic and went late into the night. Given his long hours, that may not mean anything. Zach scrolled back through the weeks. McCrae had accessed the records of several of the names on Whittaker's list, but nothing suspicious.

Ah...then, again. Zach stopped scrolling. Four weeks ago, McCrae had accessed Deb Parker's medical records. Only—Deb Parker wasn't his patient.

Of course, he may have just been asked for a consult. Zach groaned. Maybe he was going about this the wrong way. He opened the audit menu and clicked on Show by Records Accessed. Then, in the search box, he typed "Deb Parker," as well as the names from Whittaker's list.

Several records had been accessed by nurses numerous times a day, Alice Bradshaw among them. Presumably, those instances were to record the vital signs of hospitalized patients. The coroner had accessed Deb Parker's and Ellen Clark's records following their deaths, and so had—Zach blew out an irritated breath—Tara.

"What are those?"

Zach jerked half out of his seat at Whittaker's question.

Whittaker laid his hand on Zach's shoulder and peered closer at the screen. "Sorry, I didn't mean to startle you. You seemed so engrossed. I was curious what was so interesting."

Zach zipped the scroll button to hide the records connected to Tara. "These are audit records. I was just validating them to ensure the system is working properly."

"Chester Morton. He's one of my patients."

Zach glanced at the screen. The top line said Tara had accessed Chester Morton's file four hours ago. A patient not currently admitted. Zach hit the close icon.

"You mean you can see who's accessed records?" Whittaker pulled up a chair. "I had no idea such a thing existed. Show me how it works."

"I don't think I'm allowed to do that, sir. I'm not sure who has authority to view the logs."

"Surely, as the head of Oncology, I would. It might prove quite helpful in analyzing the distribution of care."

Zach bristled at Whittaker's keen interest. Had he spotted Tara's name? "I'm afraid without authorization, I really can't."

Whittaker stood abruptly, sending his desk chair

rolling into the wall. "Yes, I see your point. If you'll excuse me."

Inwardly, Zach fumed. What did Tara think she was doing?

He'd told her to lie low. She probably had no idea her computer activity could be tracked. Zach ground his teeth until they hurt. He never should've showed her that list of names. This was his fault.

It was only a matter of time before Whittaker sweet-talked Barb into showing him the audit trails.

Zach shuffled the cursor back and forth on the screen. It'd be so easy to turn off the audit trails for a few minutes on the pretext of making program adjustments, and then he could check the medical records himself. He clicked through the menus. One more click and he'd be in. His finger hovered over the mouse.

No, he couldn't. Everything he'd learned so far could stand up in court. If he looked at those medical records, and the action came to light, not only would he lose the case, he'd likely lose his job. And the judge wasn't about to give him a search warrant based on a hunch.

But...he could cover Tara's tracks.

Zach reopened the audit files and pulled up the records for Tara. It was impossible to entirely delete the electronic footprint, but he could bury it so deep that Whittaker would never see it, and hopefully neither would a defense attorney.

Zach tidied up Tara's records the best he could. She'd accessed and made notations on other medical records during the same computer session, so he couldn't entirely delete the log, which resulted in a time discrepancy. Hopefully, anyone looking would just assume she'd been distracted by another duty and hadn't logged off. He typed in the last of the changes and quickly logged off.

Now he needed to track her down and caution her before her good intentions got her into *serious* hot water.

The RN he'd been training earlier returned to the desk. "I have another question for you."

"What's that?"

The nurse rattled off a long-winded scenario.

Zach eyeballed the clock on the wall behind her. "I'll have to study that possibility. Can I get back to you tomorrow?"

"Oh, sure." She launched into a second question.

This time Zach made a point of checking his watch. "I'm afraid I have somewhere else I need to be right now. I'll be happy to go over all of this with you tomorrow. Okay?"

"Yes, yes. Sorry to keep you. I didn't realize...."

Zach hurried to the new wing. At the sight of Tara on the computer, his gut clenched. He should've spoken to her before making the deletions. He lengthened his stride. The nurse's station was empty aside from Tara—practically an open invitation for her to snoop.

"Tara," he said.

Down the hall, Barb stepped out of Whittaker's office looking as giddy as a schoolgirl.

Not good. "Whatever you're doing, log off. Now," he hissed to Tara, his gaze fixed on Barb.

"But I'm—"

"Just do it."

Tara yanked her pass card from the computer hub. Her hands shook from the storm she'd glimpsed in Zach's eyes before he took off down the hall. She rose, and the floor seemed to shift beneath her feet.

Zach closed in on Barb, and from the look on her face, Barb wasn't happy to see him.

But what did that have to do with her?

Zach said something, and Barb's mouth gaped open for a full three seconds. Then she exploded from her stupor. Their voices rose, but Tara couldn't make out what they were saying.

From the urgency with which Zach had demanded she log off the computer, she had a bad feeling that she was going to find out.

Zach scrubbed his forehead with his thumb and forefinger, his voice dropping to a more conciliatory tone.

Still scowling, Barb nodded and stalked off.

Tara pulled in a breath and held it as she waited for Zach to come back and explain. For a moment, she wondered if he'd forgotten about her.

Eventually he plodded toward her, his brooding gaze unreadable.

"What's going on?"

His jaw tightened in response. His gaze shifted left and then right. "We can't discuss it here."

She fisted her hands. "Then if you'll excuse me, I have work to do." She sat behind the computer again.

His gaze darkened. "Make sure that's all you do."

"What's that supposed to mean?"

Zach scanned the hall a second time and then rounded the desk. "In the ten minutes before I got here," he said, so softly she had to strain to hear him, "did you look at any medical records that you had no reason to?"

"No." She swallowed. "But—"

"I know about the but. The trouble is, I think Whittaker does, too. Now he wants to take a look at who's accessing files. He'll see that you did."

"So? I check dozens of records a day."

"Of patients not under your care?" Zach asked through gritted teeth. "If this goes to trial and the defense reviews the audit logs and sees that my informant checked medical records pertinent to my case without a legitimate reason, it will jeopardize a prosecution."

"Audit logs? What are you talking about?"

"They're like a fingerprint trail. Every action taken in a record, and by whom, is recorded in the background."

Her heart sank. "Oh."

"Yeah, *oh*."

She stared at the colors swirling on the computer

screen, and was struck by a glimmer of hope. "But I didn't tell you anything."

"No, you didn't." Hurt tinged his voice.

Great, she couldn't win here. "How do you know I didn't have a legitimate reason to look at those records?"

The tiniest spark of his usual good humor lit his eyes. "Because you just told me."

She frowned. "Okay. But you can honestly say I didn't tell you anything."

"You're missing the point." He glanced around and then leaned over her desk, his face inches from hers. "Number one—the defense would never believe me. Number two—you could be charged."

She choked on the thought. What would happen to her little girl?

A muscle in his cheek flinched. "Okay, I may have exaggerated that last part. Because I'm concerned for your safety."

Great, he was trying to scare her into staying *out* of trouble. Out of jail, no less.

She pictured herself in an orange jumpsuit. Oh, yay, she wouldn't have to worry about guys lining up for the chance to date her there. Especially the cop guy looking at her with a scowl that could strip paint. "I was just trying to help."

Zach shook his head, and the scowl disappeared. He squeezed her hand. "It's okay. I've taken care of it."

She might have thought he'd forgiven her, too, if not for the way he yanked back his hand the instant McCrae and Whittaker rounded the corner.

ELEVEN

The wind wrestled the screen door from Tara's hand as she opened it. "Has something happened?" After the trouble she'd caused Zach earlier today, he was the last person she'd expected to see on her doorstep tonight.

"Can I come in?" he asked above the sound of pelting rain.

Even if she'd wanted to say no, Suzie didn't give her the chance. She leaped to her feet, shouting, "Dak here," and tugged him inside to the toy farmyard decorating the living-room floor. "Pway wif me." Suzie pressed a plastic farmer into his hand.

Closing the front door, Tara massaged the pain pulsing at her temple.

Zach humored Suzie for a few minutes and then playfully mussed her hair. "I need to talk to your mom for a bit, okay?"

Suzie's lips dipped into a pout.

"Hey, hey, what's this?" Zach hooked his finger under Suzie's chin. "I won't play more later if you pout."

Suzie immediately brightened. "I be good."

Zach chuckled, and when he turned to Tara, they shared one of those proud looks she'd often seen parents exchange over the heads of their children at church.

She turned away and busied herself filling the kettle. Why did she have to torment herself by noticing things like that?

Because her heart had jumped to her throat at the sight of him hunkered down on the floor making farm-animal noises to entertain her daughter. Because Suzie thrived under his attention. Because, despite everything, she was ridiculously pleased that he'd come. "You want tea?" Water overflowed the kettle and poured over her hand.

He rose, a dimple winking in his cheek. "I'm good, thanks."

She twisted off the tap, left the kettle in the sink, and snatched up a hand towel. "What did you want to talk about?"

"First, I want to apologize for losing it with you this afternoon. I appreciate your help. Very much." He retrieved the laptop he'd left by the front door on his way in and brought it to the dining table. "I just got a little crazy when I thought Whittaker was on to you."

"Apology accepted."

His smile sent a rush of warmth clear to her toes. She gathered the photos she hadn't finished sorting, along with the card from Mom's neighbor, and moved them to the sideboard.

Zach caught her hand. "Sit, please."

"This sounds serious." Slipping her hand from his grasp, she sat in the chair beside him.

"I have news. I'm not sure whether it's good or bad."

She drew in a quick breath, and her heart thumped hard against her ribs.

"The coffee Alice gave you was clean. We've still got her under surveillance," he rushed on. "The fingerprint match warranted that much."

"You don't think she poisoned my lunch?"

"I didn't say that," he countered. "But we don't have a motive."

"She wants my job!"

"Maybe. But do you really think she killed Deb Parker to make you look incompetent?"

Tara ducked her head. Okay, point made. "So what's with the computer? You've decided to hack into medical records after all?"

His eyes twinkled. "Nope." He hit the power button. "Something perfectly legal. Social media."

"You mean like Facebook?"

"Among others, yes. You can find out a lot about a person that way."

"Like why they'd kill someone?"

"Maybe." He typed in a password and brought an internet browser up on the screen.

"Why do you think someone killed those patients?"

"If drug trials are being rigged, I think Alice and Whittaker might be in cahoots."

She chewed her lip thoughtfully. "That would explain why she's been at odds with McCrae lately. He's not a big supporter of AP-2000."

A tree branch scraped against the siding, making her jump. The lights flickered.

"It's just the wind."

Tara pulled her sweater tighter around her and nudged up the thermostat. "Do you really think that Whittaker or Alice would be stupid enough to tweet about their *business?*"

"No, I'm counting on the trial participants having done that." He typed "Ellen Clark" plus "Miller's Bay" into Facebook's search box. Two photos popped up.

Tara pointed to the redhead. "That's her." She scanned the wall posts, pleased to see that Ellen, like many people, allowed complete public access to her profile. "She was getting better," Tara said in surprise.

"Yes, and look at this." Zach pointed to a post farther down the screen. "Ellen pulled out of the drug trial after only one dose. She's the second patient who's shown signs of improvement *after* withdrawing from treatment."

"Do you think Whittaker killed her to make it look better for those who stay on the drug?" Tara rubbed her stomach, feeling suddenly nauseated.

"Possibly." Zach typed in another name Tara recognized from Whittaker's list. This one had no web presence. "We have the 9-1-1 call from Ellen Clark's apartment." Zach typed another name. "Detective Gray is bringing in an analyst to compare it to a voice recording I took of Whittaker."

Suzie moaned, clutched her teddy to her chest and curled into a ball.

"You not feeling good, munchkin?" Zach asked.

"Head owie," she whined.

Tara knelt beside her and felt her forehead. "She's not hot."

"But her face is cherry-red."

The roiling in Tara's stomach grew fiercer. Symptoms clicked together in her mind. Headache, nausea, abnormally flushed skin. She rushed Suzie to the window and threw up the sash. "How do you feel?" Tara asked Zach.

"Me? I have a bit of a headache."

Tara pushed Suzie's face close to the window screen. "Take big breaths, sweetie. It'll make you feel better." To Zach she said, "Turn off the furnace. Open the windows. I think it's carbon monoxide."

"Get her outside." Zach opened the thermostat cover and clicked off the heat. Then stormed down the hall to the bedrooms.

Tara could hear him throwing open windows as she dug Suzie's raincoat out of the closet. "Keep your face to the window," she said as she pulled Suzie's arms through the sleeves. Not bothering with a coat for herself, Tara grabbed an umbrella and hustled Suzie out the door.

The street was dark and a creepy feeling snaked down her spine, as if someone was watching from the shadows. Hunched against the driving rain, she urged Suzie to take deep breaths and steered her toward the safety of the car. The wind grabbed the umbrella, yanking it inside out. A flash of lightning streaked the sky. Suzie screamed. Thunder cracked the air.

Abandoning the umbrella, Tara grabbed the car door, but it was locked. Her car keys were still in the house. She scooped Suzie into her arms and dashed back to the cover of the porch.

In the distance, a siren wailed. Zach must've called.

Moments later an ambulance swerved onto the street. The fire chief arrived next in his own truck. Tara hoped the entire volunteer crew wasn't following with the fire engines. The last thing she needed was more attention drawn to her idiocy.

She never should've started the furnace before having it serviced. She shivered to think how close they'd come to being smothered by an invisible gas.

Zach emerged from the house, swept his arm around her and Suzie, and urged them toward the ambulance, where the EMTs were pulling out equipment. He hoisted Suzie into the back of the truck. "We've got suspected carbon-monoxide poisoning." He offered Tara a hand up and whispered for her ears alone, "I'll be back in a minute. I need to talk to the chief. Don't go anywhere without me."

The fervency of his concern wriggled into all the lonely places worn raw by Earl's abandonment.

The EMTs set her and Suzie on a gurney and outfitted them both with tight-fitting oxygen masks. A female EMT clipped an oxygen-saturation tester onto Suzie's finger, then checked her other vitals. The sound of the pelting rain was muffled inside the ambulance, and to Tara's surprise, Suzie immediately grew animated, delighting in all the cool gadgets and attention. It probably helped that the female EMT sweet-talking her out of her wet jacket looked a lot like Cinderella—Suzie's favorite storybook character.

Zach and the fire chief, meter in hand, passed by as they headed toward the house.

Suzie looked up at Tara with bright brown eyes, her cheeks no longer too rosy, and Tara's breaths came a little easier.

The EMT wrapped a blanket around their shoulders. "You're both going to be fine. The oxygen levels look good. But we should get your husband on some oxygen."

Tara took a second to realize the woman was referring to Zach. Tara didn't correct her. If she were honest with herself, the idea was kind of appealing. She was silly to even think it, of course. But tonight, at least, she was grateful for his solid presence. She even found herself thanking God for his protection.

Then Detective Gray's car pulled to the curb, and Tara's prayer turned to paste in her mouth. If Zach had called in the detective, it could mean only one thing.

This was no accident.

The detective nodded to Tara, then motioned the EMT to the rear door.

Tara stepped up beside her. "If this is about me, I'd like to hear."

"I was just telling the EMT that I've made arrangements for a nurse to administer a blood test here to determine your carbon-monoxide levels and, if necessary, to outfit you and your daughter with portable oxygen so you won't have to go to the hospital."

Tara swallowed her *why?* Because deep down she knew why. Detective Gray thought it'd be easier to keep her safe here than at the hospital.

"You okay with that?" he asked, as if he were giving her a choice. Which she knew he wasn't. Rain streamed down his coat as he waited for her answer.

She shifted her attention to the dark street behind him and couldn't help but shiver. "Yes, whatever you think is best."

As soon as the fire chief issued the all clear, Zach hurried to the ambulance to let Tara know. The rain had stopped, but the damp night air held an unseasonable chill. Reflections of swirling emergency lights flared in the puddles on the driveway. Curiosity seekers watched from the windows of neighboring houses. Zach shut down visions of how differently this night could have ended. *Lord, show me how to keep them safe.*

He looked up, and warmth rushed over him at the sight of mother and daughter sitting wrapped in a blanket.

"Dak here!" Suzie squealed, jumping to her feet.

An instant smile stole to his lips. Suzie's enthusiastic greeting penetrated the deepest longings of his soul, unleashing a rush of paternal feelings.

Suzie sailed into his open arms, and if he wasn't mistaken, the light in Tara's eyes suggested she'd like to, too. His pulse skittered at the thought.

He scooped Suzie onto his hip and then offered Tara a hand out of the ambulance. Once she was on the ground, he couldn't resist resting his hand at the small of her back to guide her around the puddles.

The fire chief stood at the front door, talking with Rick.

"Are you sure it's safe to go back inside?" Tara asked, the quaver in her voice squeezing Zach's heart.

"It's safe," the chief responded, but his furtive glance at Rick belied the assurance.

Suzie curled her arms into her chest and snuggled against Zach. "Me cold."

"Is it safe to use the furnace?" Tara asked.

"Come on." Zach prodded her through the doorway. "I'll explain everything inside."

The moment Zach set Suzie down, the little girl kicked off her boots and scrambled to her toy farm-yard, which now had a stream of water trickling through it.

"Oh, no!" Tara grabbed a towel and dashed to the water puddled on the floor in front of the open windows.

Zach peeled off the rain slicker Rick had given him. "I'll do that. You need to get out of those wet clothes."

She sponged at the water. "My clothes are no wetter than yours."

Zach took the towel and pulled Tara to her feet. "And I'll change as soon as Kelly gets here."

"Kelly, as in my old bodyguard?"

Zach glanced at Rick, who was still at the door, now talking with one of the officers who'd been collecting evidence. "Yes, she's back on duty." Zach tossed the towel over his shoulder and clasped Tara's upper arms. He waited for her to meet his gaze. He didn't want to tell her what they'd found. But she needed to know. She needed to be on her guard. "Tara, your furnace isn't broken. Someone stuffed a rag in the exhaust pipe."

Her gasp seemed to lodge in her throat. Her gaze flew to Suzie, and then he felt her body start to sway.

Zach tightened his hold. "Everything's going to be okay. I'm not going to let anything happen to you. I promise." His heart jolted at the vulnerability in her eyes, even as he fought the impulse to fold her into his arms.

That wasn't how a police officer comforted a witness under his protection. He knew it. She knew it. And if the hair prickling to attention at the back of Zach's neck was any indication, Gray was thinking it.

Zach gave Tara's shoulders a gentle squeeze, then released his hold. "You get into dry clothes and then we'll talk." Even to his own ears, his voice sounded gravelly.

Rick's scowl confirmed that Zach wasn't the only one who had noticed.

Before the bedroom door closed behind Tara and

her daughter, Rick pulled Zach out of their line of sight. "What do you think you're doing? She's your informant. That makes her off-limits in the romance department."

Zach let out a snort that he hoped sounded more convincing to Rick than it did to his own ears.

"Don't give me that," Rick said. "I saw the way her little girl jumped into your arms like you're her long-lost daddy."

Zach shrugged. "We've bonded. What can I say?"

"Do you honestly think I'm buying this? You might do just about anything to solve a crime, but I know you wouldn't stoop to messing with a child's affections."

Zach dropped his gaze to the toy farmyard in the middle of Tara's living room, and smiled at the memory of Suzie's *"Pway wif me."* "My affection for Suzie is genuine."

"Yeah, I know. I have eyes."

Restraining a groan, Zach scrubbed his fingers over his forehead. Rick knew better than anyone that he didn't need to do anything to persuade Tara to cooperate with the investigation, least of all befriend her little girl. But... "You wouldn't understand."

"Oh, I understand plenty. You're falling for your informant."

Zach's conscience twinged. He couldn't deny his attraction. But how could he love another woman the way he'd loved Carole? And how could he ask a woman to settle for anything less?

"Not that I blame you," Rick went on. "She's a beautiful woman with a cute kid. But look at this from her point of view. She's starved for affection, a single mom struggling to raise her young daughter alone. You come on the scene to champion her cause, to be her protector. Of course she's going to latch on to you."

Zach clenched his fist, every inch of him wanting to take a swing at Rick for characterizing her as nothing more than a husband hunter. "You don't know what you're talking about."

"I know what I see. And I know you walked away from Kim out of some commitment phobia. All I'm saying is, do you really want to break that little girl's heart when you walk away this time?"

Suzie scurried up the hallway, bundled in a fuzzy pink sleeper, her eyes bright. In one hand she clutched a bedraggled bunny, and in the other a favorite picture book.

His throat turned raw at the thought of disappointing this little girl.

Kelly's arrival spared Zach from obliging Suzie's request to read her a story, as Rick's glare pierced his back.

Kelly tossed Zach a department-store bag. "You owe me forty bucks. I hope they fit."

Zach excused himself, relieved at the chance to get out of the wet clothes that clung to him like the unbidden memories of the daughter he'd lost. Once in the washroom, he made short work of stripping out of his drenched things and pulling on the athletic wear Kelly had brought. He used his fingers to rake his wet hair into a semblance of neatness and studied his reflection. Drab gray didn't exactly do much for his appearance, but he was here to do a job, nothing more.

By the time he returned to the living room, Kelly was playing with Suzie, and Rick was sitting at the table questioning Tara.

Tara dug her fingers into the tabletop. "I know Zach said Alice didn't poison my coffee, but you must have enough evidence to arrest her now."

"This wasn't her handiwork. We've had her under surveillance since her shift ended."

"She could have done it this morning!" she retorted.

"Based on the gas levels when the fire chief arrived, that seems unlikely."

"I didn't switch on the heat until I got home. Did you talk to my neighbors? They might have noticed someone sneaking around."

Zach's heart lurched at the desperation in Tara's voice. He slid into the seat opposite her.

"Mrs. Thomas, next door, mentioned seeing your ex prowling around a few days ago," Rick said, clearly intent on gauging Tara's reaction to the implication her husband might be behind the attacks.

She shook her head. "Earl may be a jerk, but he wouldn't hurt anyone. Certainly not his daughter."

"I understand he's having financial troubles. He might've figured he'd have a valid claim to the house if both you and your daughter succumbed to the gas."

Tara's face drained of color.

It was all Zach could do to stop himself from reaching out to her. He threw his buddy a caustic glare.

Rick thumbed the corner of his notepad, his eyes focused on a smudge in the middle of the table. "I'd like to move you to a safe house until we catch this guy."

Zach watched helplessly as Tara wrestled with her emotions, her eyes turbulent.

When she didn't protest, Rick waved Kelly over. "Call and make the arrangements."

Kelly punched a number into her cell phone and leaned against the sideboard, but when she put the phone to her ear, a strange expression flitted across her face. She drew the phone down and back again, her attention fixed on the screen.

"What's wrong?" Zach asked.

"Some kind of interference."

Zach scanned the sideboard for electronics that might throw off a signal, and halted at the sight of Tara's flowers. He'd checked them thoroughly for evidence of an explosive, but…not a listening device.

He circled the table and examined the blooms again. With how minuscule electronics were these days, he wasn't sure he'd recognize a bug if he saw it.

"What are you looking for?" Rick asked.

Zach put a finger to his lips.

Instantly Rick's expression tensed. He scrawled on his notepad and turned it in Zach's direction. *A bug?*

Tara gasped. She pointed to the florist's card on the sideboard. A ladybug pendant was pinned to the corner.

Zach moved it close to Kelly's phone.

She gave him a strange look and then seemed to realize what he was doing and nodded. She finished the call quickly. "I'm sorry." Her face flushed. "It never occurred to me to check…." Her voice trailed off at Rick's silencing glare.

Zach pried the pendant from the card, but couldn't see an easy way to examine its innards. That would have to wait for the tech guys. In the meantime, maybe they could use the bug to their advantage.

"You could try playing a radio to help Suzie fall asleep if she's giving you trouble." Zach winked at Tara and snatched up her portable radio.

"Oh, yeah," Rick chimed in. "I have a buddy who does that for his kids all the time."

Zach turned on the radio and set it along with the ladybug in the laundry room. Then he strode back to the dining area with a wide grin. "Looks like we might have our first big break."

Confusion rippled Tara's brow. "Mr. Calloway sent those flowers. How could he—?" She pressed curled fingers to her lips and shook her head. "It doesn't make any sense."

Rick punched a number into his cell phone. "I'll have the department run a background check on him."

Zach waited for him to finish his call. "Whoever's monitoring that device can't be far away. The range of those things isn't that great. Or he's got repeaters set up somewhere. Either way, he must've overheard Tara and me talking about the investigation tonight and gotten scared we were getting too close. I suggest we keep the bug in play and use it to lure him into the open."

"How?" Tara wrapped her arms around her middle, looking way too vulnerable for Zach's peace of mind.

Maybe this wasn't such a great idea. He glanced to Rick, who was nodding, no doubt contemplating the same plan.

"We identify the location of the safe house where we're moving you," Rick said.

"But then we won't be safe!"

"You won't be there," Zach explained. "We'll send a decoy."

Kelly leaned back against the cupboard and folded her arms. "Do you really think this guy's stupid enough to try to take her out at a safe house?"

"If we make the opportunity impossible to resist, yeah, I'd say he's desperate enough," Zach replied.

"How are we going to do that?" Tara asked, finally sounding more like her usual, determined self.

"We name a location," Rick jumped in. "We admit it doesn't offer much protection, but say that'll it be safer than here."

"And that by tomorrow, we'll be able to arrange a more secure location," Zach added.

A this-could-work smile toyed with the corners of Rick's lips. "We'll detail exactly where she's to sleep in the house and where the two-man security detail will be. Then we set up a perimeter to ambush the guy when he makes his move."

"Sounds like we could pull this off," Kelly admitted.

Rick thumbed through the address book on his phone. "I'll make the arrangements. Zach, you get these two—" He glanced over his shoulder at Suzie asleep on the floor. "Get these three ready to move."

Zach rubbed his hands together. "Okay, Tara, you'll need to pack a couple of bags for you and Suzie. Kelly, you'll be impersonating her, so arrange your hair in the same style. Borrow a coat and a suitcase. And bundle a couple of pillows in a blanket so it looks like you're carrying a three-year-old. It'll be too dark for anyone to see the difference."

"If she's pretending to be me, where are Suzie and I going?"

Rick clicked off his phone. "That's where it gets tricky. We have to assume someone's watching the house. Zach could pull his truck into the garage so the two of you can duck into the back, but it'll look suspicious."

"Not if Kelly sits in front pretending to be Tara," Zach suggested. "I can drive her to the safe house while you follow. Once we're there, Suzie can duck out of her car seat, and Kelly can carry what looks like Suzie wrapped in a blanket into the house."

"That could work." Rick looked to Kelly, who nodded agreement.

Zach turned his full attention to Tara. "Once I drop off Kelly, you'll have to keep Suzie down until I'm sure we're not being tailed. Then I'll drive you to a secure location outside of town."

Tara's teeth dug into her bottom lip, but Zach could read the questions in her eyes.

"Don't worry, Tara. You'll be safe. You have my word." The promise stuck in his throat. He'd once made a similar pledge to his wife. He prayed this time God honored his promise.

TWELVE

Light from a streetlamp swept across the cab of Zach's truck. Heart pounding, Tara adjusted the blanket meant to hide her from view. The truck rumbled over the uneven road, and with her cheek pressed to the seat, she felt every dip. She flexed her toes and tried to shift into a position that would relieve the pins and needles piercing her leg. Thank goodness, Suzie had slept through this crazy escapade.

"We're almost there," Zach said from the front seat.

A moment later, the truck came to an abrupt stop.

Tara jerked forward, causing the blanket to slip. Peering between the front seats, she could make out a small bungalow. Would Mr. Calloway really come after her here?

Tara couldn't fathom how he'd be connected to the deaths at the hospital, or imagine any other reason he'd want her out of the way. Of course, if things went as Zach and Detective Gray hoped, they'd soon have their answers.

Zach and Kelly climbed out of the truck, and as rehearsed, Zach opened the rear door. He unlatched

Suzie from her seat and tucked the slumbering child under the blanket with Tara. "Stay down," he whispered. "I'll be right back." Next, he lifted a bundle of blankets beside the seat and handed them to Kelly as if Suzie were wrapped inside.

Kelly adjusted her stance as though the bundle was heavy. In the dim light, cloaked in Tara's hooded rain jacket, her face partially blocked by the blankets, Tara had to admit her own mother might mistake Kelly for her daughter.

Zach gently clicked the door shut, plunging her and Suzie into darkness. Tara tugged at the edges of the blanket to ensure they were fully hidden. Zach's distinctive scent clung to the fleecy fabric, mingling comfortingly with the fragrance of Suzie's baby shampoo. How many times had he bunked under this blanket on a stakeout?

Had he kept watch outside her house, too?

The possibility filled her with warmth.

When she was Suzie's age, she used to imagine God watching out for her. If she could imagine Him caring about her with half the earnestness she'd heard in Zach's promise to protect her, she might still believe God was paying attention. She wanted to. But what if Zach's plan didn't work?

Remembering something a patient had recently said—that worry is our way of trying to control God instead of allowing Him to guide our life—Tara closed her eyes and prayed.

An engine roared. The sound sped toward them.

Tara tensed. Where was Zach?

Shouts of "Down! Down!" pierced the air, followed by an explosion of gunfire.

Tara threw herself over Suzie. Terror shrieked through her body as shattered glass pummeled the blanket.

"Mommy!" Suzie cried.

"Shh, it's okay, sweetie. Mommy's here."

More engines roared to life. Brakes screeched. Then the crunch of metal against metal followed by shouts of "Drop your weapon!" ricocheted through the cab.

Cowering, as small as she could make herself, Tara clutched Suzie to her chest. "Shh, shh, shh," she whispered.

A single gunshot split the air.

Biting back her own scream, Tara covered Suzie's mouth. "It's okay, baby girl. It's okay." *Please, God, let it be okay.*

The shouts died away. Emergency lights strobed across the cab, penetrating their cover. Was it safe to get out? Would Zach come for her?

She heard muffled voices, but couldn't make out what they were saying. "Don't make a sound," she whispered to Suzie as she eased her hand from her daughter's mouth and shifted to peek out the window.

Headlights crisscrossed the front yard. At their center, Kelly lay motionless.

Tara bit back a cry.

On his knees at Kelly's side, Zach tore at her coat.

Tara's medical training overruled the surge of panic.

She edged higher and peered over the backseat. A man lay facedown on the street, his hands cuffed behind his back. Two police officers had guns trained on him. The remaining officers weren't ducking behind cover, so it must be safe.

Tara cupped Suzie's face. "Honey, I need you to stay right here. Someone's hurt and Mommy needs to help. But then I'll be right back. Okay?"

Suzie's wide eyes filled with tears, but she clutched her bunny to her chest and nodded.

"Good girl. Don't move. I'll be right back." Rather than open the rear door and expose Suzie, Tara crawled between the front seats and slipped out the driver's door. Before leaving the cover of the truck, she scanned the area one more time for signs of danger. Seeing none, she dashed toward Zach and Kelly.

Three steps from the porch, someone caught her arm and pulled her about-face. Rick. "What are you doing out here? Wait in the truck."

"I'm a nurse. They need my help." Not waiting for his response, she whirled back to Kelly and Zach. "Where was she hit?"

"The chest. Her vest should've taken the shot, but—" Zach ripped the Velcro, and Kelly's eyes burst open.

She let out a gasp, and frantically tore at her Kevlar vest. After prying it loose, she collapsed back with relief. She'd have a whale of a bruise, but the bullet hadn't breached the vest.

Zach rose and immediately swayed on his feet.

Tara's gaze locked on his bloodstained sleeve.

Rick must have seen it at the same time, because he pushed Zach down to sit on the porch step. "I'll help Kelly. You let Tara take care of that arm until the paramedics get here." He pressed a first-aid kit into her hands.

Zach's relieved expression morphed into a dark scowl. "I told you to stay in the truck."

Anger that he'd let himself get hurt ambushed her. "You also said you'd be right back." She ripped away his torn sleeve. The bullet had only grazed his flesh, but it had left behind a nasty-looking gash. She poured a liberal amount of rubbing alcohol onto a wad of cotton. "This is going to sting."

He caught her hand before she touched his arm. "Where's Suzie?"

"In the truck."

He snatched up one of Kelly's blankets and rose to his feet. "Grab the kit. We'll do this there."

He flung the blanket over his shoulder, and at the sight of two bullet holes, Tara couldn't muffle the cry that tore from her throat. Her daughter! That could have been her daughter!

Zach pulled her close. "I'm sorry. I never should have brought you here."

Stricken by the anguish on his face, she looked away. In the street, two cops pulled the gunman to his feet.

"At least now we'll get some answers," Zach said gruffly, following the direction of her gaze. "Do you recognize him?"

In the darkness, she couldn't make out his face, nor did she recognize the long, stringy hair or emaciated build. "No." Tara shivered. He was an utter stranger. Why would he want her dead?

The man doubled over.

"We need a gurney over here," an officer shouted.

Suzie's face appeared in the side window of Zach's truck cab, her thumb wedged in her mouth.

Tara rushed forward. Opening the door, she pulled Suzie into her arms. "I'm back, sweetie. It's okay. See, Zach's here, too."

Suzie's eyes didn't brighten as they usually did whenever she spotted Zach. Instead, she buried her head in the curve of Tara's neck. Tara hugged her close and offered Zach an apologetic smile.

His broad chest under the gray sweatshirt rose and fell as if fighting for enough air. Deep worry lines grooved his forehead as his gaze shifted from Suzie to her. "I'm sorry," he rasped, the edge of pain in his voice making the words barely more than a whisper.

"It's okay. We're okay." No matter that he'd driven them into the middle of this gunfight—she could never blame him. Not when all he'd wanted to do was protect her and Suzie. And for the first time, she realized that she didn't blame God, either.

With any luck, the shooter's arrest would put an

end to the nightmare they'd been living. She rested her cheek against Suzie's soft hair, and hoped against hope that tonight's events wouldn't haunt her dreams.

Rick brought over a paramedic and pressed a set of keys into Zach's hand. "As soon as Jack here says you're good to go, you can use my car to take Tara and Suzie to the hotel."

Tara surveyed the line of police vehicles and the shooter being loaded into an ambulance. "Is that still necessary?"

"Yes. We don't know if this guy was acting alone or as a hired gun. And until we have answers, we're not taking any more chances."

"The shooter didn't make it." Rick strode past Zach into the motel room.

"What? But last night the doctor said the operation to remove the bullet was a success."

"Yeah, well, the kid didn't wake up from the anesthetic."

Zach slammed a fist into the wall.

Rick took a seat on the sofa wedged between the window and bed. "I want Tara back at work."

"No way!" Zach glanced at the door adjoining Tara's motel room, and lowered his voice. "There's got to be another way."

"We've been over this. Someone at the hospital hired that shooter. His cell phone had two calls from the hospital coinciding with the first shooting and the carbon-monoxide poisoning. You said yourself that as long as this guy thinks Tara can identify him, he'll try again."

Zach's gut clenched at the reminder. As a cop, he knew Rick's plan was their best shot at convincing the guy to back off and buying themselves some time, but that didn't mean he had to like it.

Rick leaned back on the sofa. "If Tara talks about how this punk we took down was the one she saw in Parker's room, and says the police figure he came after her because he was afraid she could identify him as the perp who's been stealing drugs and peddling them on the street… I think our man will believe it."

"And what if you're wrong?"

"You can watch out for her at the hospital. We'll keep her house under twenty-four-hour surveillance. We'll keep her safe."

Zach plowed his fingers through his hair and paced. "That's what we said about last night's plan."

"Yes, and it worked. Tara and her little girl are tucked safe and sound in the next room."

Yeah, right. They might be safe for the moment, but seeing Tara pull her daughter from his glass-strewn backseat had left him completely unraveled. He'd driven around an hour longer than necessary before bringing them here last night, because he couldn't bear the thought of letting Tara and Suzie out of his sight, even if they'd be in the next room, miles away from any threat. Especially when his gut told him the threat was as real as ever.

"I don't buy that our shooter died of a surgical complication."

Rick tip-tapped his finger on the sofa arm. "It happens."

"But what if it didn't just *happen?* If the killer could finish the shooter off so discreetly, what's to stop him from doing the same to Tara?"

"He'd have done it already. The important thing is he believes that we *believe* the shooter died of complications. Or more importantly, that Tara believes it."

"Believes what?" Tara stepped through the connecting doorway. Her damp hair was splayed across her shoulders, and the fragrance of her shampoo swirled Zach's senses into a daze.

Her sudden appearance hadn't given his heart enough time to prepare. The instant their gazes connected, his legs went rubbery. Yeah, okay, maybe he was falling for his informant like Rick had accused. Lying awake last night, listening for the slightest sound of trouble, had given him plenty of time to examine this overpowering compulsion to protect her. "Is Suzie still asleep?"

"She's eating the granola bar and orange juice we picked up last night, and watching a cartoon." Tara returned her attention to Rick. "Believe what?"

Rick explained as Zach poured Tara a cup of coffee from the pot he'd brewed.

She sunk onto the corner of the bed. "So let me get this straight. Last night's shooter used the same gun that was used outside my mom's, but you don't think he had anything to do with the patients' deaths."

"Correct. He was clearly an addict. We found a bottle of oxycodone in his jacket pocket. Given the calls and the suspicious way he died, we believe that the person responsible for the patients' deaths paid this guy to silence you, and then killed him so he couldn't talk."

"That addict didn't just shoot at *me* last night. He shot at my daughter!" Tara launched to her feet and paced to the connecting door, where she peeked in on Suzie. She lowered her voice. "If you think someone at the hospital hired this guy to kill me, how can you possibly ask me to go back there? I won't be a piece of bait in whatever crazy new scheme you're cooking up."

"That's not what I'm suggesting." Rick's even tone grated on Zach's already-shredded nerves. "We'll leak to the papers that we believe the shooter killed Parker when the man caught him stealing drugs from his wife's room. Then, if you go back to work and act pleased that your suspicions were vindicated, whoever's behind this will no longer consider you a threat."

Tara sank onto the corner of the bed once again. "You *think?*"

Rick scraped his jawline, clearly hedging. "As long as you appear to be in hiding, he's going to assume you know something."

"If I knew something, you'd have arrested him by

now!" She clutched the bedspread into a fist. "This theoretical killer of yours obviously isn't playing with all his marbles. And how does my going back to work help you catch him?"

"It might not. But we're counting on him lowering his guard once he thinks we've closed the investigation."

Zach nudged her hand and offered her a coffee.

She cupped the mug in her hands as if the warmth would chase away the chilling reminders of last night. "What do *you* think we should do?" The look in her eyes—open, trusting, desperate for reassurance—glued him to the spot.

He lifted a lock of her hair, rubbing the silky strands between his thumb and fingers before sweeping it off her shoulder. Her shiver made him wish he could varnish the truth. "I think we should send you on a long vacation until we bring this guy down."

She let out a humorless laugh. "I'm beginning to wish I'd taken you up on that the first time you suggested it. Because, at this point, I'd become a waitress in Timbuktu if that's what it takes to keep Suzie safe." Her gaze shifted to the window.

Outside, autumn colors looked spectacular against the brilliant blue sky. Squirrels scurried from one tree to the next in what looked like a frolicking game of tag, reminding Zach of the game he'd shared with Tara and Suzie. He stopped short of reliving the kiss he'd stolen that day. Tara and Suzie should be outside playing now, carefree. But until they figured out why this punk had come after her, they didn't dare take that chance anywhere near Miller's Bay.

She turned from the window. "I feel safe here... with you."

His heart swelled at the admission, especially knowing how difficult it was for her to trust anyone's promises after the way her husband had trampled her heart.

"I can understand if you want to lie low for a while," Rick interjected. "We can certainly arrange for safe accommodations. But I need Zach back in the hospital. To close this case, we need more evidence to connect the shooter to the patients' deaths, or to connect him to the real killer."

Zach hated the idea of leaving her. She'd surprised him last night by asking him to pray with her before turning in. How could he walk away when she was just beginning to trust him? And beginning to find her way back to trusting God?

"What do you know about the shooter?" Tara asked Rick. "Was he a patient at the hospital? Did he have relatives there? And where does Mr. Calloway fit in?"

"We're looking into all those questions."

Suzie called from the other room.

Tara set down her mug and headed for the door. "Then I'd just as soon wait here and see what answers you come up with."

Rick clicked the door shut behind her, then faced Zach. "Vacation? What was that about?"

"I don't want to see her in harm's way."

"You've never had any trouble letting any other informant take risks."

"She's not any other informant," Zach said tersely.

"Yeah, I can see that."

"Can the innuendos. Tara's not a criminal trying to get out of a conviction. She's a concerned citizen trying to do the right thing. A concerned citizen with a three-year-old daughter to protect."

Rick balled a sofa pillow between his palms, the same way he'd palm a basketball in the middle of a game of pickup when he had something on his mind. Something personal. Something Zach wouldn't want to hear.

Zach turned away and gulped back the last of his coffee. It had a bite as bitter as the one he sensed his buddy was about to take out of him.

"Why didn't you tell me you were a widower?"

Zach's head jerked around so fast his neck muscles clenched. "Who told you that?"

"Tara."

He nodded stiffly. What was there to say?

"So is that why you don't date anymore? You don't want to lose anyone else?"

Zach set his coffee mug on the table. Then he pocketed his wallet and keys, his back to Rick.

"Why didn't you tell me?"

Zach glanced up and met his buddy's gaze in the mirror. "Because I didn't want to have this conversation."

"Hey, I understand. If I lost Ginny, I'd be afraid of

risking my heart again, too. But it looks to me like you're already halfway there with Tara."

"That's not it at all."

Rick lifted a brow. "Isn't it?"

Okay, maybe it was. He'd convinced himself he couldn't love another woman, but how else did he explain what Tara was doing to his insides? "We're not discussing this."

Rick bolted off the sofa. "Fine. It's your life. Probably just the kid making you so soft, anyway."

In that single tick of time, the image of his own baby girl flashed through Zach's mind, perfect in every way, and with the memory, a floodgate opened.

"I'm going to the office to follow those leads." Rick opened the door leading to the corridor. He didn't know about the child Zach lost. He couldn't know. If he did, he wouldn't be so heartless.

"As soon as Kelly gets here, I want you back at the hospital." Rick paused, as if he expected an argument. Then he walked out, leaving Zach questioning every feeling he'd experienced since meeting Tara.

THIRTEEN

The next morning, Tara snagged the complimentary newspaper from outside the motel door while Kelly hit the shower. An inch-high headline proclaimed, Police Shoot Hospital Bandit.

What?

She scanned the article, hopeful her nightmare was over, only to realize the article was a fabrication—the very information Detective Gray had proposed leaking. But why would he do that when she hadn't agreed to play along?

The instant Kelly stepped out of the bathroom, Tara thrust the article at her. "How could they do this? My family and friends will be frantic when they read this. It says I was shot."

Kelly patted the air in a calming gesture. "It says you were shot *at*. And don't worry—Zach assured your sister you were safe. She went looking for you at the hospital yesterday after your neighbor asked her about the ambulance in your driveway."

Tara reached for the phone. "I have to call her."

Kelly pressed the disconnect button. "We should talk first."

"Susan needs to know what's going on. What if this guy tries to get at me through my family?"

"He's not going to draw that kind of attention to himself."

Tara crossed her arms over her chest. "How do you know?"

"From what we've pieced together, he likely only intended to scare you into keeping your mouth shut."

"He poisoned my lunch."

"There wasn't enough poison to do more than make you sick," Kelly countered.

"Maybe he didn't know that. He must've seen that I didn't eat it. Why else would he send that shooter after me the same day?"

"As it turns out, your shooter was ex-military, a crack shot before he got wounded and addicted to pain meds. If he'd intended to hit you that night, he would have."

"Is that supposed to make me feel better?" Tara smoothed the blanket covering her sleeping daughter and lowered her voice. "Because, in case you didn't notice, he didn't have any qualms about smothering me, and my child, with carbon monoxide. Or shooting to kill you."

Kelly snorted and rubbed at her bruised side. "Trust me. I noticed."

"What did Mr. Calloway say about the flowers and ladybug?"

"He said he didn't send them. We had him under surveillance within twenty minutes of discovering the bug, and he didn't so much as make a phone call." She paused. "But the shooter's cell phone has a record of a call from an unidentified number within minutes of our laying out the safe-house plan for the benefit of our ladybug listener."

"Then who sent the flowers?"

"We don't know. It was a cash purchase. The florist doesn't remember taking the order, figures her part-timer must have. But that woman is away on her honeymoon. A place in Niagara Falls sells the ladybugs, but they sell dozens a week. Mostly cash sales, too."

Tara paced the length of the room. "Calloway could be lying."

"It's possible. But when the local paper reported that shooting, they included an interview with Calloway, who they identified as a neighbor. Anyone could have seen that and called himself Mr. C, hoping you'd simply assume the flowers came from Calloway."

"I can't stand this." Tara grabbed a sofa pillow and hugged it to her chest as she lowered herself into the room's lone chair, a wingback. "We can't just hide out here indefinitely."

Kelly slipped back into the bathroom without comment, probably feeling the same.

But how can I go back to work and risk this guy coming after Suzie? Tara stroked her daughter's tangled hair, grateful that at least one of them had been able to sleep. Every time she closed her eyes she heard the gunshots, saw the blood seeping through Zach's sleeve.

Curling her legs under her, Tara shook away the image. But she couldn't erase from her mind the sight of Zach's soulful eyes when he'd told her he had to leave. One half of his mouth had turned up in a sad smile as he'd assured her that Kelly would take good care of her.

His obvious reluctance had felt nice. Really nice.

Suzie had launched into his arms, and a moment later, so had she.

When Zach wrapped his arms around her, and rested his cheek against her hair as if he might never let go, she realized that she didn't want him to, either.

Zach had pretended to snatch Suzie's nose between his fingers, drawing a giggle, then he'd turned his smile to Tara and brushed his thumb along her chin. "Take care of yourself," he'd said softly.

No, Zach would never put Suzie in harm's way.

Tara shifted her gaze to the window. She'd thought Zach would come back in the evening, but he hadn't. And as she lay awake in bed, she'd found herself praying again. Praying that God would make sense out of everything that had happened. Praying He'd keep Zach safe. Praying He'd make it safe for her and Suzie to return home. And she'd felt a peace wrap around her as real as Zach's comforting arms.

But she didn't think she could stand another day with nothing to look at but these four walls.

"Suzie has never been the target. You've got to see

that." Kelly came out of the bathroom with her hair pulled into a ponytail, and rolled the newspaper in her hand. "Otherwise this guy would've used her as leverage a long time ago. Suzie's been caught in the crossfire because of her proximity to you. That's all."

Tara tightened her hold on the pillow, sickened to think her daughter was in danger simply by being near her. "What should I do? What would *you* do?"

"Is there somewhere Suzie could stay for a while? Your sister's maybe?"

"We going Auntie Susan's?" Suzie squealed, bouncing up and down on the bed.

Tara's heart jumped to her throat. She sprang to her feet, dropping the pillow into the chair. She hadn't realized Suzie was awake and dreaded to think what else she might have heard. Tara pasted on a smile and caught her daughter in a bear hug. "Would you like that?"

Suzie squirmed free and bounced more. "Yes. Yes. Yes."

"Mommy couldn't stay with you."

"Wanna go Auntie's."

Tara threw Kelly a helpless look.

"I really think it's the best way, Tara."

Tara let out a sigh. "I suppose you're right."

It took all morning for Kelly to clear the change in plans with Detective Gray, but by one o'clock, with Suzie settled at her sister's, Tara finally made it to the hospital.

Zach met her at Kelly's car with a welcoming smile. He opened her door. "Good to see you back."

"Thanks. I think." He hadn't shaved in a couple of days, and Tara decided she liked the effect.

He tucked her hand into the crook of his arm, never taking his eyes off her face.

There had to be a dozen reasons why she should slip her hand free, but she couldn't think of a single one. All she could remember was how good it had felt to be in his arms. As if he'd needed to hold her as much as she'd needed to be held.

"You'll be fine." He slipped something into her pocket and then, still holding her hand, turned toward the hospital.

"What's that?"

"A two-way radio. If anyone so much as looks at you the wrong way, all you have to do is press the button and I'll find you."

"Wow, my own remote-control knight in shining armor. Cool."

"We aim to please." He chuckled, the deep, throaty sound bringing a rush of warmth to her cheeks. "How's Suzie?"

"Good." Tara shook her head. What was she doing?

She'd promised herself she wouldn't drag Suzie on an emotional roller coaster. She shouldn't be letting her heart trip at Zach's nearness.

The front doors of the hospital yawned open.

Her gaze drifted up the drab, gray wall to the fourth

floor. She should be checking herself into the mental ward to have her head examined for being here at all.

A car barreled into the parking lot behind them.

Tara spun to look, only to have Zach rush her out of harm's way.

"It's Melanie's fiancé!"

Jeff parked across two parking spaces and had his door open before the engine stopped. He pulled open the back door and struggled to lift someone out of the seat. Zach and Tara sprinted over to lend a hand. An ambulance blocked the E.R. bay doors, justifying Jeff's erratic parking job. He emerged from the back-seat with Melanie in his arms, and from the way she shivered despite the mass of blankets wrapped around her, it looked as though her fever had returned with a vengeance.

Tara commandeered a wheelchair, then fast-tracked the woman through triage and into a bed. As the nurse on duty tucked a heated blanket around the shivering cancer patient, her fiancé spoke frantically. Tara wished the nurse-in-charge had allowed Zach to come in, too.

"I didn't know what to do. The shivering got so bad, I couldn't get her warm." Jeff moved to Melanie's side and brushed her perspiration-drenched bangs from her forehead. "I'm sorry, Melanie. I know you didn't want to come, but I got scared."

"Has she taken anything to bring down the fever?" Tara asked.

"Oh, no. She—"

Melanie's glassy eyes met Jeff's with an inexplicable urgency.

"She…" Jeff hesitated. "She wanted me to call her doctor first. But I couldn't get a hold of him."

"I'll send word to Dr. Whittaker that she's here. I'm sure he'll come down the first chance he gets."

Something akin to panic lit Melanie's face. "No, Dr. McCrae. Please."

Tara patted Melanie's covered foot. "I'll go up to the ward and find him for you myself." As Tara left the room, Betty, at the desk, flagged her down. "That hunky computer guy told me to let you know he had to get back to work, but to call him if you needed him."

"Thanks." Tara figured Zach would want to know how Melanie was doing, but she hated to use the two-way radio he'd given her unnecessarily.

"How is she?" Zach's voice sounded behind her, as if just thinking about him had made him materialize.

Suppressing a smile, she turned. "Stable. It'll take a while to bring her temperature down, and even longer to figure out what caused it to spike."

Zach cupped her elbow and led her to a quiet corner out of the flow of patients and staff. "Is she complaining of any other symptoms? Sore throat? Cough?"

"No."

"She didn't take anything?"

"Jeff said she refused, until she could talk to her doctor. And what was even weirder, when I offered to send Dr. Whittaker down to see her, she panicked. She asked for McCrae instead." Tara dropped her voice to a whisper. "Do you think Whittaker did this to her?"

Zach gave her arm a reassuring squeeze. "She would have said so."

"I don't know.... I don't like it. Ellen and Debra's symptoms started with a high fever. If Jeff had delayed bringing Melanie in any longer, she may have started seizing, too."

"Okay, if the nurse will let me visit with them now, I'll see what I can find out. Are you heading up to your ward?"

"Yes, Betty called up to let them know why I was delayed. But I have to find Dr. McCrae first. I promised Melanie I'd ask him to come down and see her."

Zach glanced back to the desk. "Why didn't they just page him?"

"I got the impression Melanie didn't want Whittaker to know."

"Interesting."

Tara took the elevator upstairs. Rushing off to D ward, she collided with Dr. Whittaker.

"Whoa, there." He caught her arm to keep her from stumbling, only his grip didn't feel nearly as comforting as Zach's had. "Miss Peterson? I didn't realize you were back."

His curious expression didn't seem menacing, but with Melanie's panicked look fresh in Tara's mind, she stuttered over an explanation. "I'm…uh…looking for Dr. McCrae. Have you seen him?"

"In his office, I believe. Anything I can help with?"

"Thank you, no. Excuse me." She hurried toward McCrae's office before Dr. Whittaker could ask any more questions.

"This case is getting stranger by the day." Zach glanced across the truck seat at Tara as he drove her home. The air had cooled considerably and dusk had fallen. "Melanie was sleeping when I tried to see her, and Jeff didn't want to talk about what happened. He was really shaken."

"Has Melanie started an alternative treatment? Do you think that's what caused her fever?"

"That's what I'm wondering. It would explain why she didn't want you to call Whittaker. She knows McCrae is more supportive of the alternative treatments."

"So it's a coincidence that she presented with the same symptoms as Ellen and Debra Parker. Debra had been in the hospital for more than a week. She couldn't have been slipping out to go to some alternative-treatment facility."

"Hmm." Zach turned into Tara's driveway, and the truck's headlights swept over the front porch.

Tara grabbed the dash. "Did you see that?"

Zach shifted into Park and peered through the windshield. "What?"

"On the porch. I saw something move." The wobble in her voice constricted Zach's chest.

There were no cars on the street. Kelly wasn't here yet. It had to have been Tara's imagination, a trick of the light. Shadows clung to the walls. Suddenly one shadow detached itself.

"See." Tara pointed at the figure racing off around the side of the house.

Zach yanked his flashlight from the glove compartment. "Lock the doors and wait here." Flicking on the light, he ran to the end of the house and peered around the corner. The unlit backyard, canopied by a giant oak and edged by a thick hedge, offered too many places for an intruder to hide. Every cell in his body rocketed to high alert.

He listened for movement. Nothing.

After a quick glance over his shoulder to make sure Tara was staying put, he edged along the side of the house, scanning every shadow with his light. New dead bolts wouldn't deter someone determined to get in. The thought stole his breath. If he couldn't find this guy—

He cut off the thought. Not finding him wasn't an option. He never should have agreed to let Tara come back. But he'd thought the guy would back off. They'd been monitoring her house since the night of the shooting, and no one had come skulking around looking for her.

Zach circled the yard, listening for the slightest sound. But not even the wind whispered through the trees. Slowly, he made his way around the house, checking for signs of an attempted break-in, or sabotage. Again, nothing.

Satisfied that the prowler was long gone—for now—Zach returned to the truck.

"There's no sign of him. But we'll find somewhere else for you and Kelly to stay."

Tara unsnapped her seat belt. "No. I won't let Dr. Whittaker scare me out of my own home."

"Whittaker? You saw him?"

"No." Tara climbed out of the truck. "But if you'd seen how panicked Melanie looked when I offered to get him for her…"

Zach hurried Tara to the cover of the porch. It surprised him how calm she sounded. He would have thought that coming home to a prowler would freak her out a little more than this, but, then, he'd come to expect the unexpected from her. He supposed that, like cops, nurses quickly learned how to not fall apart in an emergency. His admiration for her went up another notch, even as he tried to assess the situation and how he was supposed to keep her safe.

He'd start by asking Gray to put a tail on Whittaker.

Zach took her key, unlocked the door and surveyed the room before stepping aside so she could enter. Except, once in the light, he could clearly see how shaken she was. He pulled her into his arms. Her shudders rippled through him, and his heart ripped open as silent tears dampened his shirt. "Shh, it's okay," he murmured, when the situation felt anything but.

FOURTEEN

Tara melted into Zach's arms, absorbing his strength. She wasn't used to having someone in the middle of a crisis focus on her well-being. And she was tired of fighting. Fighting to stay out of a murderer's sights. Fighting to protect her daughter and her job. Fighting her attraction to Zach.

For just a minute, she savored the warmth of his arms. The steady beat of his heart beneath her cheek was remarkably comforting. She drew in a deep breath, and with it, the hint of leather clinging to his shirt. Part of her wanted to stay here forever.

He relaxed his hold and gripped her upper arms. "Maybe we've overlooked the obvious."

"The obvious?" She glanced around her living room. Suzie's toys were strewn on the carpet. A half-empty mug of cold coffee sat on the end table. A couple tins of wall paint were stacked in the corner, waiting for the redecorating job she'd planned to finish weeks ago. But nothing obvious jumped out at her.

"Your ex. He's already snuck around once that we

know of. He likely stole the key you had hidden and expected to be able to let himself in without a problem. The man is out of a job and desperate for money. You're an easy target who probably wouldn't press charges even if you caught him."

She planted her hands on her hips. "Of course I would."

Zach cupped her cheek and gave her a crooked smile. "No, you wouldn't. You're too softhearted."

The tenderness in his voice turned her knees to jelly.

"Not to mention, he's Suzie's father and, knowing you'd do anything to protect her, he wouldn't let you forget it."

At the thought of Earl using Suzie to manipulate her, Tara gritted her teeth. "You're right." She hurried to her bedroom and opened her jewelry box. The broach was still there.

Zach hovered at the doorway. "What is it?"

"A broach that Earl's mother gave Suzie. He asked for it back, but I refused."

"Unfortunately, without catching him in the act, we can't know for sure the prowler was him."

"Oh, I can tell when Earl's lying." Tara grabbed her coat. "Come on...let's go."

Zach caught her arm. "Maybe you should let me talk to him alone."

"Absolutely not. I can read in his face what he's *not* saying. You can't."

Fifteen minutes later, they cornered Earl in his

garage. The hood of his soon-to-be-repossessed car was still warm. "Tara, what are you doing here?" Wariness, not surprise, tinged the question.

"Be happy I didn't send the cops. What did you think? That I wouldn't change the locks after you came prowling around the first time? How stupid do you think I am?"

He held his hands up, all innocence. "I don't know what you're talking about."

For an instant, Tara believed him. Then she noticed the twitch in the corner of his eye. She pulled her cell phone from her pocket and punched in a couple of numbers. "So you won't mind if I call the police to rule out a match of your fingerprints."

Earl glanced toward the open garage door, looking ready to bolt.

But Zach stood with his arms crossed over his chest, blocking the exit. "You should've worn gloves," he said in a matter-of-fact tone, as if they had undeniable proof of his guilt.

At the sight of sweat popping out on Earl's brow, Tara pressed her lips together in grim satisfaction. "How could you scare me like that?"

"You're talking crazy." Earl turned to Zach. "I'm telling you, she's always coming up with these whacked-out ideas. If I was a minute late getting home, she'd be calling the hospital thinking I'd gotten into a car accident."

Zach's nostrils flared. "Ever think that maybe that was because she cared about you?"

Earl snorted. "You say that now, but try living with her."

His words slashed through Tara's heart, slicing open scarred-over wounds, leaving them stinging and raw. She'd tried so hard to love him, to be a good wife and mother.

The garage went deathly silent. The reek of oil clutched at her throat. A lone light bulb flickered, too weak to push back the cold darkness that crept through the windows and door.

Then Zach's voice, low and steely, rumbled through the silence. "Tara is the most selfless, caring, intelligent woman I know."

Tara blinked at the fierce sincerity in his voice. His strong hands curved around her shoulders, drawing her from the darkness that had begun to swallow her. Instinctively, she tried to pull away, but Zach wouldn't let her go. His grip was gentle, but firm, holding her at his side.

"You were her husband," Zach growled at Earl. "You vowed to honor and protect her. *Cherish* her. Do you even know the meaning of the word?"

Earl glared at them in defiance.

Thrashing past her pain and humiliation, Tara squared her shoulders.

"Answer her. How could you scare her like that?" Zach demanded.

Earl, a good eight inches shorter than Zach and fifty pounds lighter, actually cowered.

Staring at Earl now, Tara wondered if she'd ever really loved him, or if she'd fallen in love with the idea of being loved, being married, being out from under her parents' roof. But she couldn't bring herself to hate him. He'd given her Suzie, and for that she would be eternally grateful. "You were there. We know you were."

His shoulders rose and fell in vague assent. "No law against that. I didn't steal nothing. You changed the locks."

"So sorry to have messed with your plans." Part of her wanted to have him hauled off to jail on the spot, but all she could hear was Suzie's teary voice the first time she asked why she didn't have a daddy like the other kids. Suzie deserved better than a jailbird for a father. "Is that how you want our daughter to know you? As the guy who robbed our house? I don't ever want to find you sneaking around my house again. Do you hear me? Or I *will* call the police."

At his sheepish nod, Tara went limp with relief.

Zach curled his arm around her shoulders. "Come on, I'll take you home."

You're falling for your informant. Rick's words whispered through Zach's mind.

He glanced across the truck at Tara. Her hair glistened under the passing streetlights. Watching her stand her ground against her ex-husband as she'd grilled him about the attempted break-in, Zach had found himself moved beyond admiration. Then, when Earl had berated her, it had taken every ounce of self-control not to haul back and sock the weasel in the mouth.

He couldn't bear to see Tara hurt or afraid or in any kind of danger—the same way he'd feel about any woman on his watch. Only, the emotions that had charged through his chest hadn't felt the same at all.

He pulled into her driveway and shifted into Park, but she made no move to climb out. He may have relieved her fears that her attacker was on the prowl again, but Earl's verbal attack had left her shaken.

"You okay?"

She shrugged. "I keep wondering what I could've done differently."

"With Earl?"

"Yes."

The depth of guilt Zach heard in her voice was staggering. Considering how long she'd likely been shouldering the blame for Earl's abandonment, it was a miracle she hadn't self-destructed.

He turned her gently toward him. She tried to hide her pain, but he could see it in her deep brown eyes, could feel it in her almost imperceptible wince. "Tara, Earl has remarried. You can't undo that. You can only move forward from here. Don't let regret over the past steal your *now*."

She dropped her gaze. "I know I shouldn't."

"But it's easier said than done," he added.

"Yes."

"You have so many admirable qualities." Zach lifted her chin. "Don't let Earl make you think otherwise."

She let out a good-humored snort.

Smiling, he trailed his thumb along her bottom lip. The sudden thought of waking every morning to her smile filled him with unspeakable joy. He pictured them chasing their children in a lively game of tag. He heard Suzie call him Dad, not Dak, and the sound arrowed deep into his heart.

Tara looked at him, her soft eyes soothing all his ragged edges. She was so much more than he ever thought he'd have again. And suddenly all that mattered was convincing her that she deserved more, too. "You are a special woman. You deserve better."

The doubt in her eyes raked over his soul. More than anything, he wanted to be the man who made her feel truly cherished. Safe. Protected. Her long lashes swept down over her cheeks, moisture clinging to the feathery wisps. He trailed his fingers along her jaw, curled them beneath her hair at the nape of her neck, and gently touched his lips to hers.

Her eyes opened, and she went still. Very still.

His heart thumped hard.

Then she closed her eyes, and to his utter amazement, her hands slipped around his waist, and she kissed him back.

He drew her to himself, deepening the kiss. She tasted of sweet autumn breezes and the air after a storm. He lost himself in the wonderment of this precious woman welcoming his embrace. When he slowly pulled back, she let out a soft sigh.

He touched his forehead to hers. "Believe me, Earl left you because something was wrong with *him,* not *you.*"

The living-room light splashed across the front yard. Then instantly disappeared as the drapes fell back into place.

Tara sprang away from him. "Oh, my, Kelly's already here. She must have parked in the garage."

Zach restrained a groan. He'd stepped over the line. Gotten carried away. But even knowing that he hadn't acted professionally, he couldn't scrounge up an ounce of remorse.

Tara reached for the door handle. "We'd better get inside before she wonders what we're doing out here."

Zach rounded the truck to escort her. After the way Earl had treated her, he couldn't blame Tara for being skittish.

Kelly had the door open by the time they reached the porch. "Everything okay?"

"We spotted Tara's ex prowling around the place and went to have a chat with him." Zach met Kelly's scrutiny square on, not about to apologize for what she may or may not have seen him and Tara doing.

The corner of Kelly's mouth quirked knowingly, and of course, one look at the becoming flush of Tara's cheeks would confirm her suspicions.

He allowed himself a moment to revel in how right

Tara had felt in his arms, then forced himself into cop mode.

Kelly's laptop sat open on the dining table, so he hoped she'd already made some headway in finding out what treatments might cause a fever, as he'd asked. He helped himself to a slice of pizza from the open box on the table and scanned the web page on the computer screen.

Kelly quickly hit a key that cleared the screen.

Zach swallowed his bite of pizza. "Hey, I was reading that."

She flashed him a silencing glare before turning a concerned expression to Tara. "Your sister called. She wants you to call her back."

"Oh." Tara glanced at the clock. "I didn't realize how late it was. I promised I'd call and talk to Suzie before bedtime. Excuse me." She hurried to her bedroom, and the door clicked closed behind her.

"Okay, now do you mind telling me what that was all about?" Zach took a seat in front of the laptop and pulled up the web page she'd hidden.

"There are some things that Tara's safer not knowing. If you were thinking straight, you wouldn't have to ask."

Shifting in his seat, Zach read the screen.

Letting out a huff, Kelly took the seat beside him. "Coley's Toxin is the most promising possibility I've found. The treatment induces a fever that's supposed to trigger the immune system to fight the cancer."

"Widely used in North America in the early twentieth century until the government outlawed the concoction in the seventies," Zach read aloud. "Interesting."

He set down his pizza slice and looked up Coley's Toxin on Google. The search landed another interesting hit. "Look at this. A cancer patient is blogging about a treatment that he claims is helping him make a spectacular recovery."

Kelly read over his shoulder. "An injection of staph and strep bacteria? Sounds nasty. No wonder the government banned it."

"It induces fevers that are short-lived but ferocious. Sounds a lot like what Melanie had."

"If she was on this stuff, that would explain why she'd refused medicine to help bring down the fever."

Zach tried to track the blogger's profile. "The information's blocked." He skimmed through the blog posts. "He doesn't say where he's getting this stuff or what it's costing him."

"Check the comments section," Kelly suggested. "People tend to be more chatty there."

"Yes!" Zach clicked on the profile of a Chester. "He's from Niagara. He's got to be the same guy whose name is on Whittaker's list. Now we're getting somewhere."

"I thought you said Melanie explicitly asked that Whittaker *not* be summoned?"

"He could have warned her not to draw attention to him."

Zach returned to the Google search and found a

cross-reference to Coley's Fluids, a more stringently consistent version of Coley's original formula.

"Hey, get this." Kelly pointed to the screen. "The stuff is produced by a private biotech company right here in Canada, but patients who want the treatment have to travel to Germany or Mexico."

The mention of Mexico jogged Zach's memory. "McCrae's brother went to Mexico for an alternative treatment. McCrae was pretty steamed over the lack of approval for similar treatments here."

"If McCrae referred Melanie to an illegal treatment facility, it would explain why her fiancé didn't want to talk to you about her treatments."

"Except this afternoon wasn't the first time she had a fever. She had one in the hospital last week. And... McCrae supported her refusal to take something to bring down her fever."

Kelly glanced over at him. "You think he's the one running a sideline in alternative treatments?"

Zach scraped his fingers over his gritty eyes. "I don't know. This is pure speculation. We have no proof."

"It makes sense, though. When people get desperate enough, they'll pay anything for another chance."

Yeah. He knew what that felt like. When Carole's fight against cancer had headed south, he'd been ready to grab at any hope the doctors would offer. Is that what was going on at the hospital? Was McCrae preying on patients' fears of death by offering a miracle cure? Or was Whittaker trying to play God, and luring McCrae into unwittingly supporting the illegal treatment…by exploiting what had happened to his brother?

Down the hall, the bedroom door opened.

Kelly pushed the laptop closed, then leaned near his ear. "Think about it. He'd swear the patient to secrecy. But if the patient started seizing, a spouse might threaten to expose him."

Oh, yeah. A compelling motive for murder.

Kelly straightened as Tara joined them.

"How's Suzie?" Zach nudged the pizza box in Tara's direction, shaking off the direction of his thoughts.

"Good." She glanced from Kelly to him to the closed laptop. "Any luck with the research?"

"Nothing concrete," Kelly responded before Zach had a chance.

Tara slumped into the chair opposite Zach and picked at a pepperoni slice. "Nothing at all?"

The disappointment in her voice niggled at his conscience. He shot a sideways glance at Kelly, who gave a slight shake of her head. He knew she was right. The less Tara knew of their suspicions, the less likely she'd be to say or do something that might tip off their suspect. He reached across the table and stroked Tara's hand. "We're close. This will be over soon."

"By tomorrow?" Her gaze lifted to his. "My sister has to fly to Calgary to interview some oil tycoon for an article."

"Can't she do that by phone?"

"The guy refuses. So Susan's editor wants her to

take advantage of the opportunity and fit in other interviews while she's there. She'll be gone a couple of days."

"Couldn't Suzie stay with your mom?" Kelly asked.

"No way," Zach and Tara said in unison.

Tara gave him a surprised look.

"It would rouse bad memories of the afternoon you were shot at."

"Yes."

Kelly cleared her throat.

Zach jerked his attention back to her. Oh, boy. He needed to get a grip. One glimpse of Tara's eyes and he lost all sense of professionalism.

"Is there a friend you feel comfortable leaving Suzie with?" Kelly pressed.

"No. Suzie's never stayed anywhere but at my parents' and Susan's. Am I going to have to go back into hiding?"

Zach shook his head. "I don't think that's necessary." By tomorrow, he might have convinced Melanie to give up her supplier. In the meantime, he'd have McCrae and Whittaker put under surveillance. "Suzie will be safe in the hospital daycare while you're working, and either Kelly or I will be with you the rest of the time."

"Detective Gray also has regular patrols going past the house," Kelly added.

"The same patrols that kept my ex from sneaking onto the property tonight?"

Kelly bit her lip, dropped her gaze.

"You're right." Zach covered Tara's hand with his own. "It's easy enough to sneak past a patrol car. But your ex won't come around anymore, and I honestly think you've fooled our suspect into believing he's safe. If you suddenly take more time off, though, he could get worried. Besides, when you're here, you will have protection inside the house with you. Kelly will be here when I'm not."

"You really think Suzie will be safe with me?"

The anxiety in Tara's voice made Zach's chest ache. "You've got to know that I wouldn't do anything to put your little girl in harm's way."

FIFTEEN

In the hospital parking lot the next morning, Kelly tripped the automatic door lock as Tara started to climb out. "You'd better wait. I don't see Zach's truck here yet."

Tara glanced at the dashboard clock. Six twenty-five. "He'd better hurry. My shift starts in five minutes."

Kelly pulled out her cell phone and punched in a number.

Warmth rushed to Tara's cheeks at the thought of seeing Zach again. Not that he'd been far from her thoughts since last night. The sparkle in his eyes. The smile lines at their corners. The dimples in his cheeks. If only her ex-husband's cruel insults hadn't tainted the memory of Zach's sweet words and even sweeter kiss.

Her insides trembled. Zach's interest seemed serious. Really serious. And that scared her.

Kelly snapped shut her phone. "He's on his way."

Tara's breath backed up in her chest. She wasn't ready to face him. Not yet. She thumbed the lock switch open. "I'll head up to my floor, then. Don't want to draw more attention to myself by being late."

Kelly scanned the parking lot. "Yeah, okay. I'll let him know."

As Tara rode the elevator up to the cancer ward, she wondered what it would be like to be cherished by a man like Zach. She wasn't naive enough to believe her quirks wouldn't drive even someone as sweet tempered as Zach a little crazy. But part of loving someone was overlooking those kinds of things. At least that's what Susan had kept insisting on the phone last night after she'd dragged out of her all the details of their romantic parley.

Tara leaned against the elevator wall and closed her eyes. She could still feel the warmth of Zach's strong hands steadying her as she'd faced Earl. She hadn't realized how much she'd been trembling until Zach's touch had grounded her. And then there was the sincerity in his voice when he'd told her something was *wrong with Earl,* not *her.*

The elevator doors slid open. Alice Bradshaw and Dr. Whittaker stood a few feet away, heads bent over the clipboard Alice held. What was Dr. Whittaker doing here so early?

Alice glanced up as Tara stepped off the elevator, and immediately shifted her stance, blocking from Tara's view whatever the pair were poring over.

"Good morning," Tara said with as much pleasantness as she could muster.

Neither betrayed any indication they'd heard her.

But the way Alice steered Whittaker into the privacy of the alcove raised Tara's guard.

She slowed her step as she neared them.

"There's got to be another way to convince her to mind her own business," Whittaker whispered.

The air froze in Tara's lungs, but somehow she forced her suddenly boneless legs to keep moving. With each step her spine stiffened, along with her resolve. She wouldn't be bullied into turning a blind eye to what had gone down in Debra Parker's room. Mr. Parker had begged her to stop the killer. A dying man didn't make stuff like that up.

Tara rounded the corner of the nurse's station and collapsed into the desk chair, her mind reliving the moments before his death. She could see it clearly now. Whittaker, Bradshaw and McCrae had all rushed into the room in response to the code blue. They'd worked feverishly on Mrs. Parker...or at least that's how it had appeared. Not one had come to her aid to try and save Mr. Parker. She'd assumed that his gaze had been pinned to his wife when he'd begged her to stop the killer. But what if he'd been looking at the very person he feared would finish his wife off?

"You okay?"

Tara shook the images from her head and shifted her attention to the departing RN. "Yes, sorry. My mind was somewhere else." She tucked her trembling hands under her thighs.

The RN filled her in on a few minor changes in

their patients' conditions and then gathered her coat and purse.

"Wasn't Melanie Rivers readmitted last night?" Tara asked as the woman headed out.

"Nope. No new admissions."

Tara reached for the phone. With a quick glance to where she'd last seen Alice and Whittaker to ensure she wouldn't be overheard, she dialed the E.R. extension. "Hi, Beth, this is Tara on D ward. I'm checking on the status of our cancer-patient Melanie Rivers. She came in yesterday with a high fever. Do they want to admit her?" Tara heard papers shuffling on the other end of the line.

"No. Looks like you're off the hook. They sent her home."

Sent her home? From the way Melanie had looked yesterday afternoon, Tara had expected to find her seriously ill this morning. As she hung up the phone, a shadow crossed over her desk.

Tara's heart jumped into her throat. "What are you doing here?"

McCrae chuckled. "Haven't you heard? I live here."

"You pulled another all-nighter?"

He sloughed off her exasperation with a shrug. "Thanks again for coming to find me to see Miss Rivers yesterday. Your concern for your patients does you credit."

"I still don't understand why she wouldn't take anything to bring down the fever until she saw you."

"Fevers are the body's natural defense mechanism. She was letting it do its job." Admiration tinged his voice.

"You mean you didn't give her anything for the fever, either."

His eyebrow lifted, in silent censure. "Are you questioning my judgment?"

"No, but..." His tone had sounded affronted, but the twinkle in his eye said he was teasing. "Well, yes. Yes, I am. She could have suffered brain damage."

"We monitored her temperature closely and, since we were able to keep her comfortable with warm blankets, we decided to let the fever run its course." He rested his hip on the edge of the desk and clasped his hands over his knees. "Not conventional, I know. But the strategy worked equally as well. Perhaps better. Wouldn't you agree?"

Tara squirmed under his penetrating gaze. "No, I would've been more comfortable with giving her meds."

McCrae chuckled. "Well, at least you're honest."

Tara straightened the files on the desk, avoiding eye contact. Although they'd occasionally engaged in small talk, she'd never seen McCrae this...*interested* before.

"Don't you wish sometimes that you could do more?"

"More?" She rummaged through the desk drawer for a stapler.

He stilled her hand with a fleeting touch. "To help your patients?"

"Oh—" She had a weird feeling this was some sort

of test, and that no matter how she answered, she was going to be in trouble.

"Take yesterday, for example. Miss Rivers told me you offered to fetch Dr. Whittaker."

"Yes, but she wanted to see you."

"Because she knows that I have her best interests at heart. I think you'd agree that sometimes Dr. Whittaker is more concerned with..." McCrae's hand fluttered, as if trying to pluck just the right word. "...other things."

Tara's arm jerked, knocking a stack of files askew again. Restraightening them, she stole a glance at McCrae. What did he mean? Did he know what Whittaker was up to?

"I can see you're not like that." McCrae thumbed through the stack of files and pulled a couple. "From here on out, I hope I can count on you to trust my judgment."

She stared after him, vaguely uneasy about how to interpret his unexpected alliance. A call bell startled her attention back to her duties. She smoothed the creases from the file she'd been clenching, and left the desk to see to the patient.

As she took the elderly woman's blood pressure, she caught sight of movement at the door, followed by a light tap.

"Everything okay?" Zach's voice drifted into the room.

Turning, Tara breathed in the scent of fresh soap

and leather. His hair was still damp, the curly ends brushing the collar of his jacket. "Yes. Thank you."

His gaze dropped to her lips, and her stomach did a little flip. "I'll be nearby if you need me." The huskiness in his voice raised pinpricks of awareness on her arms.

She nodded, not trusting her own voice.

He wavered a moment longer as if he might say more, then slipped away.

"Your beau?"

Startled by her patient's question, Tara spun back toward the bed, and the blood pressure cuff she'd stopped pumping halfway inflated. She deflated the cuff to start again. "No, just a friend. Sorry for the interruption."

The woman's eyes twinkled. "A friend? That's not what he thinks."

Tara's heartbeat hopscotched around her chest. Dare she believe it might be true?

She'd been so affected by his appearance, she'd forgotten to tell him what she'd overheard Whittaker say this morning.

A couple of hours later, Dr. Whittaker slapped a printout onto her desk. "Why didn't you tell me Melanie Rivers was the reason you came to get McCrae yesterday?"

Tara's stomach tightened. "I was in a hurry."

"I bet. And afraid of being reprimanded for contaminating another IV."

"What are you talking about?"

He speared his finger into the printout—Melanie Rivers's lab report. She had elevated levels of both staph and strep in her bloodstream. *The same bacterial combination found in Ellen's bloodstream after her death.*

"You're blaming me for this?" Tara's voice rose.

Dr. Whittaker looked pointedly at the sweater she'd thrown on over her scrubs. "Isn't that the same sweater I see you wearing when you pick your daughter up from daycare?" He twanged the sleeves. "Infection, Miss Peterson… Do I have to remind you what will happen if the press gets wind of a story like this? The fallout would be disastrous."

Tara forced herself to take a full breath. This couldn't be what it looked like. Whittaker would *not* want word of this to get out. A good thing, too, because it looked like he'd set her up as a scapegoat.

Zach's pulse rocketed at the beep of the two-way radio he shared with Tara. He excused himself from the nurse he'd been instructing on the new computer system and checked the radio's GPS. It showed Tara in almost the same position as his, but at a lower elevation—the daycare. She'd made arrangements for her sister to bring Suzie there this morning.

He sprinted to the back exit and barreled down the stairs to the main level. He hit the hallway at the same moment Tara stepped out of the daycare with Suzie perched on her hip.

"Dak!" Suzie squealed.

Hauling in a breath, he closed the distance between them. Both Tara and Suzie looked fine. So why had she beeped him? "You okay?"

"Yes, we're just waiting for our ride." Her head tilted and her smile lost some of its wattage. "Why?" She glanced around and lowered her voice. "Is something wrong?"

He jiggled Suzie's foot and grinned. "Not if you're okay. Suzie must have sat on the radio in your pocket."

She boosted Suzie a little higher on her hip. "Oops. Sorry about that."

"I'm not complaining. Just glad you're okay." The sound of another email alert on his cell phone boosted his mood even higher. After learning that Melanie hadn't been admitted to the hospital, he'd decided that tracking her down at home might raise too many suspicions. So he'd set up an email address under the alias Lucy Baker and struck up a conversation on the blog he'd found last night. Figuring most guys were more willing to help a woman than a man, he'd asked where *she* might get the treatment he was taking, and listed the email address to win the blogger's trust and to encourage a private, detailed response.

He glanced at the message. *Yes!*

Through a flurry of emails, he'd finally gotten the guy—Samuel Adams—to trust *Lucy.* Now he'd agreed to a meeting.

"Excuse me a second," Zach said to Tara, and keyed in *Lucy's* agreement. Now all he and Rick had to do was find a female officer to pose as Lucy Baker—their dying cancer patient.

Tara nudged him away from the front of the daycare center. "There is one thing I need to tell you. I overheard Whittaker tell Alice that he needed to find another way to convince me to mind my own business."

"When?" Zach bit out the word.

"First thing this morning. Then later he insinuated that I was to blame for Melanie's infection."

"Melanie has an infection?"

Tara ducked her head, probably realizing she'd inadvertently breached confidential information.

"What kind of infection, Tara? I need to know."

She glanced around nervously. "Staph and strep, just like Ellen."

Staph and strep, the two main bacterial strains in Coley's Fluids. That clinched his theory. He clearly should have paid more attention when Gray had reported Ellen's autopsy results.

Before he could ask for more details of Whittaker's threat, the man sidled up to them and tickled Suzie's chin. "Hi, there. Good to see you feeling better."

Suzie tucked her head against Tara's shoulder.

"You playing shy?" Whittaker sported a playful frown. "Kids never like the doc."

Zach fought the urge to show him that kids weren't the only ones. The man oozed charm like a tube that didn't know when to stop.

"Dak not a cop," Suzie exclaimed.

Zach forced out a laugh, but Tara's face blanched.

"That's right," Dr. Whittaker agreed, "doctors aren't police officers." To Tara he added, "You've got a bright one here."

Tara's cheeks went from white to pink. "Thank you."

Dr. Whittaker continued down the hall a few yards and then stopped to chat with a couple of nurses.

Spotting Kelly at the door and not wanting to press Tara for details on Whittaker when the man was within earshot, Zach said, "Can we talk later?"

"Yes, come for dinner."

The rush of words seemed to surprise Tara as much as they surprised him. He'd been to her house almost every evening since starting this case, but she'd never offered him a home-cooked meal. "I'd like that very much. Around six?"

"Yes." The breathless catch to her voice made his heart hitch.

"Bye, Dak," Suzie squealed.

Whittaker glanced over his shoulder with a wide smile. "Bye, Suz—" His gaze shifted to Zach, and the instant cock of Whittaker's head said he realized his mistake. Would he realize Suzie's earlier "Dak not a cop" comment hadn't referred to him, either?

Zach's mind reeled through potential explanations. They were on the verge of uncovering a link between the hospital and illegal Coley's Fluids treatments. The last thing they needed was his cover blown.

Tara's sudden intake of breath didn't help matters.

Whittaker's smile lost its brightness, but he hesitated only a moment before turning away.

"Whew," Tara mouthed, except Zach wasn't so sure they'd dodged the bullet. Suzie had inadvertently tipped his hand, which meant if Whittaker had a guilty conscience, he'd be watching *both* of them more closely than ever.

SIXTEEN

"Me stir, Mommy," Suzie begged as she plowed a kitchen chair toward the counter.

Tara tied a waist-style apron around her little girl's shoulders, and the frill still reached the seat of the chair. Tara showed her how to hug the bowl of cake batter with her arm to keep it steady and then handed her the whisk.

"Like this?"

Tara swept a curl out of Suzie's eye. "Yes, honey, you're doing a good job." Seeing her daughter's enthusiasm, she chided herself for usually waiting until Suzie's nap time to bake. Although she suspected Suzie's enthusiasm had more to do with Zach coming than baking, unlike Kelly, who'd been unusually quiet since learning of their plans.

Tara brushed the fine dusting of flour off Grandmother's recipe card, wishing she could shrug off Kelly's unspoken censure as easily. "You're going to love this cake, sweetie. My grandma and I used to make it when I was little. It was my favorite."

"Dak gonna love, too." Suzie scooped a hunk of batter onto her finger and licked it. "Mmm, yummy."

Tara tickled Suzie's belly. "Hey, you've got to stop taste testing or you'll be too full for dinner."

Giggling, Suzie hunkered down, guarding her belly from Tara's tickly fingers.

Soon the aroma of baking cake filled the house. They shooed Kelly and her laptop to the living room and set the table with their best linen tablecloth, good flatware and fancy crystal tumblers.

"Look, Mommy." Suzie pointed to the rainbows splashed on the tablecloth from the sunshine touching the glass.

Tara couldn't imagine a more perfect day.

The conversation she'd overheard between Alice and Dr. Whittaker infiltrated her thoughts, but she shut it down. She wasn't going to let anything spoil their special night with Zach.

She pressed her palm to her fluttery tummy. He wasn't at all like Earl. He accepted her for who she was. Yet, he wasn't afraid to challenge her about her tendency to wallow in the past. And when he held her in his arms, he made her feel unbelievably precious.

Still… After weeks of trying to convince herself she'd be crazy to start another relationship, she couldn't believe that she'd actually invited him to dinner.

Suzie set down the last fork. "Can I wear my pink dress?"

"Sure you can."

As soon as Tara finished helping Suzie put on her favorite dress, white tights and shiny black shoes, Suzie twirled around the house. "Dak come soon?"

Kelly stepped inside from her hourly patrol of the yard. "He'll be a while yet."

"Why don't you color him a picture while I put the potatoes on?" Tara suggested.

Suzie pulled out her coloring book and crayons and turned to a picture of Sleeping Beauty's handsome prince. "Dis one?"

"Sure, sweetie. Any one you like."

Suzie scrunched a chubby yellow crayon into her fist, wedged her tongue at the corner of her lips and set to work on the prince's hair—blond like Zach's. Tara smiled at her daughter's earnestness. The fear that, mere days ago, would've engulfed her at the thought of Suzie growing too attached to Zach, hovered only dimly in the corner of her mind.

Deep down she knew that Zach wouldn't hurt them.

After stopping at his apartment to change into fresh clothes, Zach headed for the florist shop next door. He hoped it wasn't wishful thinking that had him reading more into Tara's dinner invitation than just an opportunity to discuss the case, because the vulnerability he'd seen swimming in Tara's liquid-brown eyes had turned him inside out.

The bell over the door jingled as he entered the shop, and a brightly dressed woman bustled out from behind the counter. She looked his mom's age, but her caftan, with its splashes of purple, orange and yellow flowers bore no resemblance to the matronly clothes his mother favored.

She opened her arms wide. "Welcome. How may I help you?"

He pointed to a cheery bouquet of mixed flowers in the cooler next to the counter. "I'll take one of those."

Her smile fell. "Someone is sick?"

Heat crept to his cheeks. He'd taken a similar bouquet to Ginny and she hadn't hinted that he'd made some floral faux pas, but from the arch of the florist's brow, apparently he had. "No, they're for a friend."

The twinkle returned to the woman's eyes. "May I suggest roses then?"

"Oh, no. I don't want to scare her."

Laughter spilled from the woman's mouth. "They needn't be red. White roses are a symbol of caring, light pink of admiration, and my favorite—" She showed him lilac-colored rosebuds. "These tell her you're enchanted."

Oh, boy. His gazed flicked from one array of flowers to the next. "I had no idea people read so much into a simple bouquet." He scraped his hand over his chin. Maybe this wasn't such a good idea.

The woman opened the cooler and lifted out the original bouquet he'd requested. "Tell me what attracted you to this one."

"The sunflowers," he said easily. They reminded

him of Tara's sunny disposition and captivating brown eyes.

The florist's beaming smile returned. "Sunflowers symbolize adoration."

"Hmm, I like that."

She plucked the sunflowers from the bouquet and combined them with some reddish-purple zinnias.

Glancing at the clock, Zach decided not to ask what zinnias meant. Somehow he didn't think this woman would steer him wrong. Standing at Tara's doorstep fifteen minutes later, he wiped his damp palms on his pant legs and prayed the flowers weren't too much.

The curtains at the window slanted open and Suzie's nose pressed to the glass. "Dak here," she squealed and a moment later, the door burst open.

The delight on Tara's face when he handed her the bouquet sent a jolt of pleasure rumbling through his chest. She welcomed him inside, and between the sweet aroma of home cooking, and the feel of Suzie's tiny hand in his, cozy family images filled his senses.

Kelly angled past him with a chilly "Call me when I need to come back."

Letting Suzie drag him across the room, Zach scanned the windows, reminding himself of the other reason he was here. While Tara put the flowers in a vase, Suzie proudly showed him the elegantly set table, babbled happily about how she'd helped her mommy bake the cake and then twirled around the living room to show off her pretty dress.

"Could you help Suzie into her booster seat while I bring out the food?" Tara called from the other room.

She carried a platter of chicken to the table, placed a small helping in front of Suzie and disappeared into the kitchen again.

Suzie's nose wrinkled.

"What kind of face is that?" Zach teased. "Your mom went to a lot of effort to make us a delicious-looking meal."

"Don't like," Suzie grunted, crossing her arms over her chest.

"But little girls don't get dessert if they don't eat their supper."

As Tara returned carrying a pitcher of juice, a giant tear spilled down Suzie's cheek. "Dak said I can't have cake."

"The big meanie." Tara playfully bumped his shoulder. "I'm sure he was just teasing, honey. You know you'll get some."

"But not if she doesn't eat her supper, right?"

Tara nudged the plate toward her daughter. "It's chicken. You like chicken."

This time Suzie's entire face scrunched along with her nose. "Not *red* chicken."

"That's the sauce. It has ketchup and honey and brown sugar. Mmm." Tara dipped the edge of Suzie's spoon into the dish. "Try it. If you still don't like it, I'll make you a peanut-butter-and-jam sandwich. Deal?"

Suzie nodded, and Tara spooned a smidgen of the

chicken sauce into her mouth. Immediately, Suzie made a sour face and reached for her sippy cup. "Don't like."

Tara let out a resigned sigh. "Okay, a sandwich it is, but you don't know what you're missing."

"I'll say," Zach interjected, "that cake sure smells yummy."

Tara swatted his shoulder. "Stop teasing her."

"Who's teasing?"

Tara rolled her eyes and hurried back into the kitchen. A moment later she returned with a sandwich for Suzie, to which she added the tiniest spoonful of steamed carrots. "Now, I expect you to eat those vegetables."

Suzie slanted an apprehensive glance in Zach's direction.

He actually started to feel guilty for scolding her—until he realized she was doing nothing more than pushing her carrots off the edge of her plate and nudging them underneath as she nibbled at her sandwich.

Reluctant to spoil the mood by making a big deal about Suzie's picky eating, Zach redirected the conversation to their case. "Are you sure Whittaker meant *you* when you overheard him talk about making sure someone minded their own business?"

Tara's fork stopped halfway to her mouth, her knuckles white.

Okay, bad choice of dinner conversation.

Tara lowered her forkful of mashed potatoes to her plate. "He accused me of deliberately infecting Melanie. What do *you* think?"

Zach gritted his teeth at that news. What else had Tara neglected to tell him?

Suzie's wide eyes panned from Tara to him.

"Perhaps we should talk about it later."

Tara's nod suggested she'd prefer not to talk about it at all.

Zach's gaze skittered over the sunflowers adorning the center of the table as he dug into his chicken. Talking about Whittaker was *not* how he'd hoped to end his evening with Tara.

"'You turned another page,'" Zach wailed as Tara joined him in the living room.

On the sofa beside him, Suzie giggled and burrowed under his arm. Over Suzie's head, Tara and Zach shared a smile, a connection so warm and effortless that Tara practically floated across the room.

In true three-year-old fashion, Suzie seemed to have completely forgotten her hurt feelings over Zach's hard time about her getting cake. But if Tara were honest with herself, she'd have to admit that she'd suggested she do the washing up because she'd needed a little space to examine her own reaction to Zach's surprising stance.

His reaction had felt too much like a jab at her parenting decisions, but after listening to the two of them reading stories, she conceded that she'd probably been oversensitive. Thanks to Mom's continuous commentary on how she did things around here, she tended to have a knee-jerk reaction to any opinions expressed on the matter.

Zach scooched over on the couch, making room for her on his other side. In a gruffly voice, he begged Suzie not to turn the page, because that would bring them closer to the monster at the end of the book. This close, the rumble of his voice reverberated through her. Then feeling Zach pretend to quiver with fear, Tara realized she and his frightened monster had a lot in common. For the past fifteen minutes, she'd rehashed how Earl had betrayed her, worrying that Zach would do the same if she gave him the chance. Why couldn't she simply enjoy this time together and leave the future in God's hands?

She smiled at the realization of how natural thoughts about God's hand in her life had become since meeting Zach.

As if he'd read her thoughts, Zach squeezed her hand. He turned the final page of the book to reveal the same silly character smiling up at them. "'And you were so scared,'" Zach said in his monster voice.

Tara couldn't help laughing. Maybe she'd be pleasantly surprised to find that nothing scary was waiting for her around the next page, either.

The instant Zach finished reading the story, Suzie begged for another.

Tara rose to choose a short one, but to her surprise, Zach said no.

"We agreed on three. It's way past your bedtime."

He tweaked Suzie's nose. "You don't want to turn into a pumpkin."

Tara smiled to herself. Maybe he wanted their alone time as much as she did. She held out her hand to Suzie. "Zach's right. We have an early day tomorrow. Come on... I'll tuck you in."

Suzie launched herself into Zach's arms. "I want Dak to."

Zach looked to Tara for permission, and the apology in his eyes nixed the momentary twinge of jealousy her daughter's request had sparked. After all, she should be grateful that Suzie adored him as much as she did.

Tara followed them to Suzie's bedroom, where Zach prayed for her daughter. Tara's heart warmed at the sincerity and affection in his voice. Then Suzie took a turn praying. From the first day she'd met Zach, Suzie had added "Dak" to her bedtime prayer. When Zach glanced at Tara, his eyes moist, her throat clogged. Was he thinking of the daughter he'd lost?

The thought had niggled at her more than once over the past couple of weeks, and with it, a fleeting wariness she didn't want to begin to decipher.

Tara kissed Suzie good-night, and then silently led the way back to the living room.

"She's a sweet girl," he said, his voice husky with emotion.

"*I* think so. But then I'm her mother, so I might be biased." Tara grinned. "Can I get you a cup of coffee?"

He caught her hand, his grip playful but firm, and

tugged her toward the sofa. "It can wait. We need to talk."

Tara tensed at the terse edge to his tone. "I'm sorry I didn't tell you about Whittaker's accusation earlier, but I didn't think the hospital hallway was the best place."

"No, I understand. What else did he say?"

"Nothing. But I think McCrae suspects he's up to something."

Zach turned to face her. "How so?"

"When I asked him why Melanie wanted to see him instead of Whittaker, he said that Melanie knew he had her best interests at heart. That Whittaker was too distracted by *other* things."

"Did you ask him what he meant?"

"No, the implication seemed clear. Whittaker's always on the lookout for more recruits to his drug trials. And it's no secret that McCrae's not a supporter."

Zach's gaze drifted to the window, and Tara could almost see the gears turning.

"What are you thinking?"

Zach tucked a strand of hair behind her ear and then trailed his finger down her cheek, sending electricity skittering through her chest. "For your own protection, I'd rather not say."

She pursed her lips, swallowing her protest. She didn't like being kept in the dark, but she understood why he felt it necessary. "What's going to happen once you have the evidence you need?" They'd never talked about the future, yet she wanted to believe that he wouldn't leave.

He cupped her face in his hands. "You'll have to testify."

She jerked back. "That's not what I meant."

He squeezed her hand. "I know, but you need to know what to expect. The defense will try to have the evidence thrown out. They'll accuse you of feeding me information from private medical records. They'll make a big deal about our apparent relationship."

"Apparent?" The word stung. She yanked her hand free and hunkered into the corner of the couch, hugging her knees to her chest. "Is that all this has been? A masquerade?"

He gave her a lopsided grin with enough wattage to melt an iceberg. "Absolutely not. You can't get rid of me that easy."

The tension in her muscles began to ease, except... "For the past few weeks, you've been posing as an IT consultant in Miller's Bay twenty-four hours a day. Are all your assignments like this?" Embedding himself in a fake identity for weeks on end wasn't exactly conducive to a fledgling relationship, let alone a stable family life. How had she let her heart get so far ahead of her brain?

"They can be." Zach rested his hand on her knee and gently urged her to lower the legs she'd barricaded between them. "But not if I have a reason to turn the assignment down."

"Such as?"

The soft light from the lamp behind her twinkled in his eyes. "Such as, if there were someone I wasn't willing to be separated from." His hand lifted to her chin, and he brushed his thumb across her bottom lip. "Someone special," he added, echoing the words he'd used to describe her the night before. "Because I wouldn't want you to worry that I wouldn't come home."

"Hmm." She smiled. "That's good to know."

Suzie padded into the room, rubbing her eyes. "Mommy, I'm hungwy."

Tara got up from the couch and ushered Suzie to the table. "I saved the sandwich you didn't finish."

Zach caught her gaze and frowned.

Tara hurried to the fridge. Did he expect her to let Suzie starve?

Zach slipped into the galley kitchen, blocking the opening to the dining table.

Tara veered around him and set the plate in front of her daughter, then started on the coffee.

Zach crossed his arms, his frown now a scowl.

Tara yanked a couple of coffee mugs off the hooks under the cupboard. "What?"

Zach stepped in behind her and massaged her shoulders. "Nothing." His body turned toward Suzie and then back to Tara. "Nothing."

Tara tensed, despite his hands gently kneading her shoulders. "I think I know what's best for my child."

"Of course you do." His hands dropped down to her

arms and then fell to his side. Even though he agreed with her, Tara felt patronized.

Tara reached into the fridge for the milk. It was Earl all over again. Whenever he thought she'd done something stupid, he'd frown and scowl and say it was nothing when it was clearly something. Did Zach think she was a bad mother because she'd saved Suzie's supper?

She pushed past Zach with the glass of milk. "Excuse me." Suzie had scarcely begun the sandwich. "Hurry up and eat," Tara said more harshly than she'd intended.

Suzie gulped down the glass of milk and took a big bite of the sandwich.

A twinge of guilt knotted Tara's stomach. She'd been the one who'd let Suzie taste test while they'd baked. It wasn't Suzie's fault she wasn't hungry at dinnertime. But why should she have to justify herself to Zach?

Tara stole a glance over her shoulder to where Zach was still leaning against the counter, observing them with an unreadable emotion in his eyes.

"C'mon," Tara said to Suzie, "I'll take you back to bed now."

"I want Dak to."

The emotion in his gaze transformed to unmistakable affection, but he said, "You be a good girl and go with your mom. Okay?"

Suzie's bright smile crumbled.

"Hey, what's with the long face?" Tara took up

the tickle-monster pose that never failed to delight her daughter.

Squealing, Suzie scrambled toward her room.

Tara scurried after her, but before she could tickle her, Suzie clambered into bed and yanked the sheets to her chin. Tara chuckled as she kissed Suzie on the forehead.

"Mommy?"

"Yes?"

"Why Dak mad at me?"

"He's not mad at you, honey."

Suzie's bottom lip quivered. "I sorry I didn't eat my supper."

Tara stroked Suzie's hair. "I know you are, sweetie." She also knew that Zach meant well. He clearly adored her daughter. Maybe she was the problem. But after three years of defending her parenting decisions to everyone from her mother to the little old lady in the playground, the last thing she wanted was to have to defend herself to Zach.

"Dak'll come back. Won't he?"

A sigh escaped Tara's chest. Of course that would be her daughter's greatest fear. She kissed Suzie's forehead. "You don't need to worry. Okay?" Tara could worry enough for both of them. Zach's words—*I wouldn't want you to worry that I wouldn't come home*—whispered through her mind, but Earl's *You say that now, try living with her* outshouted them. Maybe she just wasn't ready to let someone else into her life, to let him have a say in Suzie's life. Maybe she'd never be.

When she returned to the kitchen, Zach offered her a cup of coffee. "Double cream, no sugar, right?"

"I've lost my appetite." She dumped the coffee down the sink.

"Tara, please—"

She shook her head and wandered to the sofa. This evening wasn't going the way she'd hoped.

Zach took the seat at the opposite end of the sofa and searched her eyes. "I'm sorry I upset you. But don't you think letting Suzie go to bed hungry and experience the consequences of her choices would've served as a better lesson than feeding her?"

"And have to listen to her whine half the night? No, thank you."

"I get that. I'm just concerned that by indulging her you're setting a precedent you'll regret."

"I do *not* indulge my daughter."

"You gave her cake for supper!"

"She helped bake it! She'd been looking forward to sharing it with you all afternoon."

His expression turned contrite. "I'm sorry. I didn't mean to spoil that for her." He closed the distance between them and reached for her hands. "You've got to know I love Suzie as if she were my own daughter."

"Are you sure that's what you're feeling?" No matter how much it might hurt, Tara needed to know the truth before she and Suzie grew any more attached to him. She withdrew her hands from his and pressed her arm against the ache building in her chest. "Because I've seen the tears Suzie brings to your eyes."

Zach bowed his head. He rubbed the bare ring finger of his left hand, no doubt remembering the wife and child he'd lost.

The ache in her chest intensified as his face contorted with pain. Stinging pricks arrowed to her eyes and throat and heart. Biting her lip, she blinked back tears.

Silence stretched between them like a widening gulf.

Why didn't he say something? Anything?

But she knew why. Because he was only in love with the idea of a family. Of recapturing what he'd lost.

Tara hardened herself against how much that hurt. As much as she wanted Suzie to be happy, they both deserved more—a man who could love them for themselves.

Before she could talk herself out of ending things, Tara sprang to her feet and grabbed Zach's coat. "You'd better go. Goodbye, Zach."

His head snapped up, confusion swirling in his eyes. "Goodbye? You're ending this?"

"Yes."

"Over chocolate cake?"

"Don't make this more difficult than it has to be," she choked out.

"It doesn't *have* to be difficult at all."

Tara clenched the leather jacket in her fist and shut down the thought that she was ending the best thing that would ever come along. "Yes, Zach, it does. You're in love with the idea of an instant family. But you can't recapture what you lost. Not at our expense. I won't let you hurt us that way."

Instead of snatching the jacket and storming out as she expected, Zach closed his fingers around hers. His gentle touch tugged at the frayed edges of her resolve. "I would never hurt you, Tara. Never."

I know, she wanted to say. More than anything, she wanted to lean into his arms and let his promise wash over her. Wanted to picture them together as a family. The words almost made it out of her mouth, too, but with Earl's taunt resounding in her head, she could only picture disaster. For a little while, she'd let herself believe Earl was wrong about her. That the problem wasn't with her at all. That maybe the worst wouldn't happen if only she'd trust Zach enough to give him a chance.

Her longing must've filled her eyes, because Zach curled her hands against his chest and gave her a hopeful smile. She wanted to offer her own in return. He'd brought to life dreams she'd never intended to resurrect. He'd made her feel that she could overcome *anything*.

Anything, except the ghost of his wife and child, that is.

For a moment, she closed her eyes and savored the beat of his heart beneath her palm—steady and strong. Then she slipped her hands from beneath his and wrapped her arms around herself. "You wouldn't *deliberately* hurt us, Zach, but you will hurt us. You will. Because one day you're going to figure out that you were only in love with a dream."

He opened his mouth as if he might refute her words—how she wished he would—but as their gazes connected, he pressed his lips into a grim line.

She held her breath. Too scared to utter a sound.

He took his jacket and walked toward the door.

Her breath swooshed out, and she had to grip the sofa to keep from running after him, telling him it was all a mistake. Because she couldn't. She couldn't risk raising Suzie's hopes another day. If Zach's leaving hurt this much after knowing him only a few weeks, how much more would it hurt a month from now?

She couldn't put Suzie through that.

Zach opened the door and looked back at her. "I'll wait in the truck until Kelly gets here."

Tara swallowed a lump in her throat. "Bye, Zach."

He nodded, sadness in his eyes. The door clicked closed.

Tara twisted the dead bolt and laid her head against the cool steel.

It was over.

SEVENTEEN

"I've got information you're gonna want to hear," Rick said with more enthusiasm than Zach could muster.

Time may heal all wounds, but eighteen hours hadn't taken the edge off the pain knifing through his chest since Tara had cut him out of her life. "Meet me at my apartment in ten."

Outside the hospital, Zach watched Tara and Suzie pile into Kelly's car, then shifted his own into Drive and peeled out of the parking lot. All day, every time he came within sight of Tara, she'd retreated into a patient's room. Not even her interest in the case had been enough to overcome her determination to stay away from him.

The first drops of rain splashed his windshield. Seconds later, the rain descended in torrents, pelting the glass so hard and fast the wipers couldn't keep up.

From the moment he'd met Tara, she'd reminded him of his wife, while Suzie had inspired dreams of what his own little girl might have been like if she'd lived. He scrubbed his hand over his face. Maybe the emotions churning inside him *were* just the by-product of a desire to recapture the happiness he'd lost.

He clenched the steering wheel. Usually, he was so careful to act in the best interest of others. Suzie's sweet voice mispronouncing his name chimed through his thoughts. Suzie liked having him around.

He gave his head a swift shake. He'd come between a mother and her daughter. No wonder Tara had gotten so defensive.

Given how her ex had treated them, Tara's concerns about his affections were understandable, maybe even valid.

Zach pulled into the lot behind the bakery. Rick drew a rain slicker over his head and jumped out of his truck. His huge grin said they were on the brink of a major breakthrough.

Good, the sooner they wrapped up this case, the sooner Zach could give Tara what she wanted—him out of her life. He took the stairs to his apartment three at a time, but was still soaked by the time he pushed through the door. He motioned Rick toward the couch that came with the place and, stripping out of his wet shirt, headed to the adjoining kitchenette to put on the kettle. "What did you learn?"

"I visited the company that makes Coley's Fluids and had a powwow with the head honcho."

Zach turned from the cupboard, mugs in hand. "And?"

"The four-hour drive paid off big-time. Turns out the company had a lot of inventory stolen a while back.

They never caught the thief, but they suspected an inside job. His secretary will email a list of employees in the morning."

Zach poured two instant coffees and joined Rick on the sofa. "Okay, I'll need search warrants to cross-reference both McCrae and Whittaker's phone records with the employees' numbers, and bank records, while you're at it."

"You're not convinced McCrae's acting alone? Whoever's selling the stuff has to be making a good haul. And a medical resident would have a load of debt to pay off."

"I know it doesn't look good for him, especially with Melanie testing positive for staph and strep, but he seems to genuinely care about his patients."

"Two of those patients have died due to complications following a high fever," Rick fired back. "Whoever's administering this stuff isn't doing it out of the goodness of his heart. And let's not forget about Deb Parker's husband."

"His autopsy didn't confirm foul play."

"Doesn't mean our guy didn't take him out."

Zach let out a heavy sigh and set his coffee mug on the scarred end table. Tara wouldn't be safe until whoever she'd startled in that hospital room was behind bars. The trouble was… "If those patients asked for the injections, whoever administered them isn't exactly guilty of murder."

"Murder, manslaughter, selling illegal substances. I'm not picky what we nail the guy for. I just want him stopped. I thought you'd be raring to rattle every cage you can find on this, since the sooner you wrap up this gig, the sooner you have an open field with your—" Rick cleared his throat in a we-all-know-what-I'm-not-saying kind of way "—informant."

"I told you. There's nothing going on between Tara and me."

"Yeah, sure. Whatever you say."

Zach threw up his hands. "Fine. Believe what you want." The pain crushing his chest must've shown in his face, because Rick instantly sobered.

"Oh, man, I'm sorry. What happened?"

"I blew it. She thinks I'm only trying to recapture what I lost."

"Are you?"

"No." He raked his hands through his wet hair. "I don't know. Maybe. She thinks when I figure out that I was only chasing a dream, I'll dump her. So she dumped me first."

"That's it?" Exasperation pinched Rick's voice. "You're just going to let her go?"

"That's what she wants."

Coffee spluttered from his friend's mouth. "Give me a break. Don't you remember what you told me when I let Ginny walk out of my life?"

"Yeah, a love like Ginny's comes around once in a lifetime."

"Yup, and you know what?" Rick jabbed a finger into Zach's chest. "You were wrong."

"Great, thanks, just what I needed to hear. Not only is my love life a nonstarter, my buddy's tossing in his."

"That's not what I meant. For eight years, you've thought you could never have another love like you shared with your wife. Am I right?"

Zach shrugged noncommittally.

"Maybe you're right. Maybe you can't. But that doesn't mean the life you make with someone new—after we close this case—can't be just as wonderful."

Zach crossed his arms over his chest. "What? Now you're my therapist?"

"It's my turn. You were right about one thing when you told me to go after Ginny. You said that one day I'd wake up and realize that God wanted to give me so much more than I was willing to let Him."

"Yeah, save the lectures."

Rick clunked down his mug and headed for the door. As he twisted the knob, he gave Zach one last disgruntled glance. "All I'm saying is look in the mirror."

That was the problem. Right from the start, Tara's big, brown doe eyes, so much like his wife's, had been what made his heart kick. She deserved better than a guy grasping at ghosts.

Tara headed to the nurse's station and caught a whiff of the woodsy cologne Zach favored. Her stomach lurched. She couldn't face him. Not yet. She reached for the nearest door. The knob turned easily, but when she tried to push inside, the door didn't budge. Feeling the walls closing in, she smoothed the shirt of her scrubs with a damp palm. Okay, she had to play it cool and not let him see how much he affected her. Yeah, right.

She rounded the corner and pretended to be engrossed in an item on the bulletin board.

A moment later, an elderly man ambled past, leaving that woodsy fragrance in his wake.

Her breath left in a rush. What was wrong with her?

She'd done the right thing. Zach might love Suzie, but he didn't love her. If he did, he would've tried to change her mind the other night. He would've refused to leave. He would've taken her into his arms and kissed her senseless, until she was thoroughly convinced that she was the only one he wanted to be with.

To think she'd actually contemplated whether she could be with him for Suzie's sake.

If only she hadn't invited Zach to dinner. If she'd just ignored his kindnesses for a few more days, they could've continued to work together to nail Whittaker, and then Zach would've been able to leave with no hard feelings.

Tara peeked around the corner. Not spotting any sign of Zach, she hurried to the nurse's station.

Dr. Whittaker cut her off. "Where's that file I asked for? I've been waiting in the patient's room."

"Sorry. I got sidetracked." Tara thumbed through the files on the desk and retrieved Mr. Scott's.

"You've been preoccupied a lot lately. It's affecting your work."

Tara raised her brows at his insinuation and crossed her arms. "Perhaps we can discuss the performance of *all* team members at our next department meeting."

He stood his ground, his eyes narrowing.

She winced at the realization that he might assume she was preoccupied with suspicions of him. "Was there anything else?" she asked, her voice more in control than she felt. When he shook his head, she sat at her desk chair and forced her attention to the data she had to input into the computer, typing blindly until he walked away.

"What was that about?" Dr. McCrae hitched his thumb in the direction Whittaker had disappeared.

"A misunderstanding."

"He's been edgy a lot lately. Have you noticed?"

"Yes, now that you mention it." She was sure McCrae knew more about Whittaker than he was saying. But he was probably worried that the extolled oncologist wielded the power to destroy his career.

Still, if she could coax McCrae to give them some solid proof, Zach's job here would be done. He could arrest Whittaker, and life would go on as usual. Well, maybe not as usual. Arresting the namesake for the hospital's new cancer wing was bound to cause some short-term chaos, but it couldn't be any worse than what the close proximity to Zach was doing to her fragile state of mind.

She set aside a file, and pulled the next one toward her keyboard to give the impression of only casual curiosity as she asked, "Any idea what's bothering him?"

Dr. McCrae ripped a requisition form from the pad on the desk. "I heard his drug trials were tanking."

"Oh…those poor patients. Is that why you advised Melanie to seek other options?"

"Who told you that?"

Tara's fingers stilled on the keyboard. Getting Dr. McCrae to implicate Whittaker was not going as she'd hoped. "Um, I think it was her fiancé." At least she was pretty sure that's who'd told Zach.

McCrae clicked open his pen, scrawled his name on the requisition form and then handed it to her. "Well, let's hope he didn't tell Whittaker. There's nothing worse than doing a good deed and having it turn around and bite you."

Tara's thoughts veered to the attacks against her. "Yes, I know what you mean." Her response came out harsher than she'd intended.

"I heard about the shooting. You're a lucky woman."

"No, not lucky. Someone was watching out for me."

"Someone? You mean God?" McCrae snorted. "Then where's He looking when people like Melanie Rivers are dying inch by inch?"

Too stunned to speak, Tara could only stare.

"Trust me," McCrae added with a knock of his knuckles on the desk. "You'll do better looking out for yourself."

A few weeks ago, Tara would have readily agreed. But watching McCrae stride down the hall, Tara wasn't so sure anymore. She'd been looking out for herself when she'd asked Zach to leave, and she'd never felt more miserable.

So much for coaxing info out of McCrae to hurry along Zach's investigation. All she'd succeeded in doing was depressing herself.

"You getting that?" Alice's voice cut into her thoughts.

"What?"

"The phone. It's already rung three times."

Tara's gaze dropped to the phone, and the red blink of the line-two button snapped her out of her thoughts. She picked up the receiver. "D ward. May I help you?"

"This is the hospital daycare. Is this Tara Peterson?"

Tara's pulse quickened. "Yes."

"You need to come right away. It's your daughter. Something's wrong."

EIGHTEEN

Zach rubbed his eyes. Looking at all these phone numbers was making his eyes go buggy. Not a single call on either Whittaker's or McCrae's home phone or McCrae's cell phone matched the number of anyone from the biotech company, or any of the victims. Whether any number matched Samuel Adams, the blogger scheduled to meet their undercover "cancer patient" this afternoon, Zach couldn't say, because he couldn't find a record of a Samuel Adams anywhere in Ontario. Not that he'd thought for a moment the blogger would use his real name.

So, either McCrae and Whittaker were too smart to make incriminating calls that could so easily be traced, or Zach was wasting his time trying to prove a connection. Not that the clean records proved anything. The calls to the shooter had originated from the hospital. If only they could trace individual extensions, or find cell-phone records for Whittaker.

Zach checked McCrae's email next, but his online activity was as nonexistent as Whittaker's.

Zach thought of Whittaker's list of patients and the

threat Tara had overheard him make against her. The ache in the vicinity of his heart sharpened. He had to stop Whittaker before he got to Tara.

Zach pushed back from the desk he'd commandeered in a quiet corner of the hospital and headed to the lobby to buy a coffee. His mind whirred through options. There had to be something they could trace. Zach pulled out his wallet to pay for his coffee and found a dog-eared photo of his wife stuck to a five-dollar bill.

"Keep the change," he said to the barista, his gaze fixed on the photo as he laid the bill on the counter. He sat at one of the tables and traced the outline of his wife's face with his thumb. The photo was faded and worn. The first few months after Carole's death, he'd pulled it out of his wallet a hundred times a day, but her big brown eyes still sparkled as brightly as ever. He squinted at her image.

Aside from sharing similarly shaped eyes, Tara and Carole actually looked nothing alike. He'd known that from the beginning, but Tara's accusations had made him wonder.

Not even their eyes looked *that* alike. Carole's radiated self-sufficiency and that infernal stoicism that had her comforting him near the end instead of the other way around. In contrast, Tara's brimmed with determination not to accept the given, and a feistiness to fight the injustice thrown in her path.

Yet, beneath that hard, protective coat she wrapped around her heart, he sensed a quiet yearning to not have to go it alone. A yearning that had called to him from the first day they'd met.

Not that it mattered now. He tucked the photo back into his wallet. She wouldn't even talk to him.

He didn't blame her, either. Her fierce protection of Suzie was one of the things he admired most about her.

Zach sipped his coffee and forced his thoughts back to the problem of tracing McCrae's calls. The man seemed to have no life outside the hospital. Although, from what he'd heard, that wasn't uncommon for medical residents. Whittaker, on the other hand, had an active social life. As head nurse for the cancer ward, Tara had to have a number where she could reach him in an emergency.

Zach downed the last of his coffee with a fresh burst of energy. Asking Tara for the number was the perfect excuse to reopen the lines of communication.

He rode the elevator to the fourth floor and strode to the nurse's station. Alice Bradshaw was the only nurse in sight. "Can you tell me where I'd find Miss Peterson?"

"Sorry, I haven't seen her since I got back from break."

The answer didn't surprise him. Tara seemed to have a sixth sense of his vicinity and would duck out of sight before he could corner her. "Perhaps you could help me. I'm…uh, updating the system's on-call database and I don't have an emergency number for Dr. Whittaker."

"Sure, it'll be his cell-phone number. He prefers that to a pager." Bradshaw ran her finger down a list taped to the desktop next to the phone. "Actually, the number listed here has been scratched out. I think I remember him saying he lost his phone."

Or changes it frequently to keep the numbers from being traced, Zach mused.

Back at his desk, he rechecked both suspects' bank records then pulled up Whittaker's home phone list one last time. His mind drifted to Tara and Suzie and a thought flickered—a mother. A mother or father would do anything to save their child...even steal.

He scanned the list of the biotech company's employees. One name stood out.

Zach pulled out his own cell phone and called Rick. "There's a Patricia Campbell working at the biotech company. Find out if she's any relation to Peter Campbell."

"Who's that?" Rick asked, the sound of computer keys already clicking in the background.

"One of the cancer patients on Whittaker's list. A patient who's been mysteriously getting better. If my guess is right, this patient's sister or wife or mother has provided Whittaker with the Coley's Fluids in exchange for treating him."

"Mother!" Rick exclaimed. "Patricia Campbell is Peter Campbell's mother. She's worked at the company for twenty-three years. If anyone knew how to slip a case of drugs undetected out of that place, she would."

"And chances are our Samuel Adams is really Peter Campbell."

"Could be. Keep an eye on Whittaker, but whatever you do, don't tip them off. *Lucy Baker* will keep her appointment this afternoon with *Samuel Adams,* and if he matches Peter Campbell's description, we'll arrest him on the spot."

"Yeah, with all the charges you could throw at him, he's bound to give up Whittaker in exchange for a deal," Zach said drily.

"Sit tight. I'll be in touch."

Zach gathered his papers and headed back to the cancer ward. Tara might not appreciate him hanging around, but he wanted to be where he could keep an eye on Whittaker, just in case Campbell managed to tip the doctor off.

Finding no sign of either Whittaker or Tara on the cancer ward, Zach asked the first nurse he happened upon if she'd seen them.

The nurse, Beth, fluttered her hand in the direction of the elevator. "Yeah, I saw Doctor Whittaker tear past me a few minutes ago. Headed for the elevator, I think."

"And Tara Peterson?"

"She ran out of here like a madwoman after the daycare called."

Zach fought to keep his paranoia in check. "How long ago was that?"

"Ten, fifteen minutes, maybe. Not long."

Zach slipped into the privacy of the alcove and checked the GPS coordinates for the transmitter he'd given Tara. The readout showed that she was in the vicinity of the locker rooms. Hesitating only a moment, he let himself in. The room was empty. But the readout was hot.

Checking her locker, he found the radio in the pocket of her sweater, hanging inside. He slammed the door shut and hurried to the elevator. He jabbed the button, but the light above the door didn't move off six. Surely Whittaker wasn't sick enough to use Suzie to blackmail Tara into silence. But that was exactly the fear strangling Zach's throat.

He raced for the stairs. On the ground floor, he blew out the door at a run and sprinted to the daycare entrance.

The woman who came to the door peered at the ID badge clipped to his shirt pocket. "May I help you?"

"I'm looking for Tara Peterson."

"I'm sorry, sir. There's no one here by that name."

"Is Suzie still here?" He looked over her shoulder, trying to catch a glimpse of the children. "Did Tara pick her up?"

The woman's fingers turned white where she gripped the door. "I'm sorry, sir. We can't give out that information." She pushed the door as if hoping he'd back away without a fight, while anticipating the worst.

He imagined he must look like a deranged ex-husband to this young child-care worker, but he didn't have time to explain. "Please, I know she came to get Suzie. I need to find them."

Another child-care worker approached carrying a ladybug raincoat. *Suzie's* raincoat. She stopped short as her gaze lit on Zach. "Sorry, I thought you were someone else."

Would Tara forget Suzie's coat? Had Whittaker been pursuing her in his haste to the elevator?

The first worker nudged Zach's shoulder with the door. "We're sorry, sir. We can't help you."

He backed out, heartened by the thought that these women wouldn't have permitted anyone other than Tara to pick up Suzie.

He tried Tara's cell phone, but got an out-of-service-area message. She didn't have a car. How could she be out of the area?

He keyed in Kelly's number, flubbing it twice in his haste. At the sound of the automated voice message, Zach snapped shut his phone. *Lord, where are they?*

The thought of losing Tara and Suzie—really losing them—ripped through his heart like a bullet.

Zach raced to the hospital's rear exit. Whittaker's Maserati sat in the end lot. McCrae's Jeep, too.

Zach ran to the security office and pushed through the door without knocking.

"Hey, you can't be in here," a burly officer said, hanging up the phone.

Zach scanned the wall of monitors looking for an image of the hall outside the daycare center. "There." He pointed to the feed he wanted. "Rewind this feed."

The guard—six-plus feet of solid muscle—blocked his view of the monitors. "You need to take it easy, sir. Tell me who you're looking for."

"A woman and her daughter are missing."

The guard scrutinized Zach's ID and a sick feeling balled in the pit of his stomach. The child-care worker must've alerted security about him.

Zach held up his hands in surrender. "Look, there's no time for two-stepping around who you think I am. I am *not* the woman's husband, boyfriend or any kind of significant other." Man, it hurt to say that. "I just need to find her. She could be in danger."

"Trust me, buddy, I've heard them all. If you think the child's been kidnapped, I can lock—"

Zach spotted Tara and Suzie on another monitor. The label said: Fourth Floor. D Ward. "Never mind... I see her." He hurried out.

Once upstairs, he headed Tara off outside the staff lounge. "What's going on? I've been looking all over for you." He gulped in air to try and catch his breath. "I thought something happened. Alice said the daycare called you."

"I need to take Suzie home and I can't get hold of Kelly." Tara didn't meet his eyes.

Suzie plugged her thumb into her mouth and burrowed her head deeper into Tara's shoulder.

"Is she sick?"

"Just upset. A couple of boys pretended to shoot each other, and she suddenly became inconsolable. She said, 'Dak shot,' and the daycare director assumed she meant her dad."

Zach's heart crunched into his ribs. He stroked Suzie's hair. "Hey, hon. I'm okay. You know that, right?"

She lifted her head and scrutinized him. Her teary

eyes knocked the wind out of him all over again. How could he let Tara shut him out of their lives when their happiness was as important to him as his next breath?

Tara hoisted Suzie a little higher and rescued her falling backpack. "I've arranged for someone to cover the rest of my shift." Tara's gaze met his for only an instant. "But we don't have a way home."

"I'll ask Rick to send someone."

Her shoulders drooped. "That'd be good. Thanks."

"Tara, I'd love to take you. Please don't think otherwise." He touched her arm, and her flinch hurt to the core. Somehow, some way, he needed to convince her to trust him, to believe his feelings for her were real and true. "I just can't leave right now."

"You don't owe me an explanation."

He steered her into the empty lounge. "Yes, I do." He quickly texted Rick and then, pocketing his phone, returned his full attention to Tara. "We're close to a breakthrough. In the meantime, I need to keep tabs on Whittaker." He shot a glance at the door, knowing he should be out there tracking Whittaker right now. But he couldn't leave Tara unguarded.

She moved toward the window, putting the table between them.

"I haven't been able to stop thinking about you." He stepped around the table. "And I realized something."

Finally she looked at him, her exquisite eyes full of sadness.

"You were right that I still love my wife." Tara's head dipped, and Zach immediately reached for her hand. "I will always love Carole, but that doesn't mean I can't love you, too." He rested his hand over hers on Suzie's back, and his heart swelled. "You and Suzie."

Tara blinked rapidly as she slowly lifted her gaze to his.

He ached at the uncertainty in her eyes. "I love you, Tara. Maybe I was afraid to believe it, afraid I might lose you, too. Then I did lose you, and it hurt more than I could stand."

She burst into tears.

He pulled her and Suzie into his arms. Tara buried her beautiful face against his chest and sobbed her heart out.

Zach stroked her hair, hoping against hope that these were happy tears.

Suzie burrowed down to look at Tara's face. "What wrong, Mommy?"

Zach's breath stilled.

Tara lifted her head, wiped her eyes on her sleeve. She looked such a mess he couldn't help but smile. When she smiled back, the air swooshed from his lungs.

"These are happy tears, sweetie." She dabbed at his damp shirt. "I got you all wet."

Zach rested his palm against her cheek. "I don't mind at all."

Her cheeks bloomed to an adorable shade of pink and she ducked her head.

"Soon this case will be over and we'll have a long talk," he said.

"You have enough evidence to make an arrest?"

"Almost. We've connected Whittaker to a biotech company that produces Coley's Fluid."

"What's that?" she asked, intrigued.

"An alternative cancer treatment. It's just a matter of time before we have enough evidence to prove he's guilty."

Whittaker stepped into the room with Alice at his side. "Who's guilty of what?"

Zach stepped in front of Tara and Suzie, shielding them with his body. "Nothing important, sir. Just talking about—"

"My ex-husband," Tara piped up.

"That's right." Zach latched on to her subterfuge. "He's reneged on child-support payments. I was just saying—"

"No, I heard you say Coley's Fluid. What is that? You said something about cancer."

Zach scrutinized Whittaker for evidence of deception, but saw only eager interest. Not good. Attempting to catch him off guard, Zach said, "It's an alternative treatment a friend of mine was looking into. Somehow it's supposed to trigger the immune system to fight cancer."

"Yes, I remember reading about that in medical school. It induces a high fever. Of course, why didn't I think of that before? It explains everything."

Alice turned from pouring a cup of coffee. "You mean Melanie's sudden fever?"

"Melanie's, Ellen's, Debra Parker's," Whittaker said.

"But who would do that?" Alice took a seat at the table. "I can see trying it, maybe. But after one patient died, who would risk another's life?"

"I don't know. I can't imagine any doctor jeopardizing his medical license to do anything so foolhardy. But it fits."

"How so?" Zach asked, feigning a casual interest, given Whittaker's unexpected candor.

"I have a number of patients who withdrew from my drug trials. Soon after, they inexplicably started to improve. I kept a list. I figured that if I could decipher what triggered the remission, it would put Memorial Hospital on the map."

"You're not taking credit for the improvements?"

"At first I thought it might be a latent effect of the drug we're testing. But this makes more sense."

Suzie fussed to be let down.

Tara shot Zach a questioning look. Zach nodded that she'd be okay, and Tara set Suzie at the table, then pulled a coloring book and crayons from her backpack.

Zach returned his focus to Whittaker. "So what will you do now?"

McCrae stepped into the room. "Hey, someone forget to tell me there was a staff meeting?"

"It's him." Alice pointed to McCrae. "That's why he wouldn't let me give Melanie Rivers something for her fever."

McCrae turned to the door, but Whittaker stepped in his path and blocked his escape. "Is that true, Doctor?"

"I don't know what you're talking about."

Zach shifted sideways to shield Tara and Suzie. Then, taking a chance on his theory, he said, "The police know about Patricia Campbell."

McCrae spun around, eyes blazing, and pinned his glare past Zach's shoulder. "This is your fault. You couldn't keep your mouth shut."

Tara's gasp squeezed Zach's chest.

"That's enough." He made a grab for McCrae, but the man pulled out a needle and jabbed the air between them.

"Stay back."

Zach raised his hands and took a single step back. "You don't want to do this."

"It beats the alternative." He maneuvered sideways, but succeeded only in getting farther from the exit.

Zach mirrored his move, keeping himself squarely between McCrae and Tara and Suzie. "You'll never get away," he warned.

Suzie bolted toward her mom, sending her chair toppling into Zach's leg.

As Zach caught the chair, McCrae lurched forward and snatched up Suzie, the needle still poised in his other hand. "Watch me."

NINETEEN

Full-blown panic squeezed the breath from Tara's lungs.

"Put Suzie down," Zach ordered.

McCrae scowled at Tara. "This is your fault."

Every motherly instinct in her wanted to lunge at him and claw out his eyes. But not knowing what was in the needle, and terrified he'd stab her daughter, Tara forced herself to stay back.

"David," Dr. Whittaker said. "She's just a child. Let her go."

For a moment McCrae wavered, looking as though he might relent. "I can't do that."

"Tell me what you want me to do," Tara begged. "I'll do it. Just don't hurt my daughter."

"Those are mighty big promises for someone who's out of options. You're just like *him*."

"Him?"

McCrae's eyes twitched and seemed to go out of focus.

"Parker. He didn't understand what was at stake. He knew the risks going in. I told him. He said he understood. But he didn't." McCrae's voice had a strained sound of reasonableness. "The treatment is helping people. But Parker threatened to expose my work. If I didn't stop him, he would've cost them their lives."

Zach inched toward McCrae's side, but Tara forced her gaze to stay focused on McCrae.

"Did you hear me? I had to consider the greater good. I thought you understood."

"Of course, the greater good," Tara repeated inanely. He seemed to be in a trance. The man was playing God with people's lives.

McCrae's eyes pulled back into focus and narrowed in on her.

"Every patient who got the treatment knew the risks. I didn't sugarcoat it. So you can see how I had no choice." He raised the hand that held the needle. "To serve the greater good, sometimes one has to make sacrifices."

Zach grabbed McCrae's arm.

Tara pounced on his other arm, Alice, too, prying it from around Suzie, as Whittaker tried to grab the needle. For a few seconds McCrae resisted, but then he released his hold on Suzie, and turning, punched Zach in the kidney.

Zach lost his grip.

Tara pulled Suzie out of the way as Whittaker and Zach tried to corner McCrae. Alice jetted around them out the door, hopefully to get help.

"Put down the needle," Zach said, his voice steely calm. "You don't want to hurt anyone. You lost your brother like I lost my wife. You didn't want to see others suffer the way we had to. I get that."

"I was trying to help them."

"You were. You gave them hope." All the while Zach talked, he, Whittaker and McCrae danced around each other, no one's eyes ever far from the syringe in McCrae's raised hand.

A security guard appeared at the door. "What's going on?"

Zach lunged at the momentarily distracted McCrae and caught one of his arms in an armlock.

McCrae steamed backward, driving Zach into the wall.

"No," Tara screamed as McCrae levered his arm down, spearing the syringe into Zach's chest.

Roaring, Zach shoved McCrae face-first to the floor.

The security guard snapped a handcuff on McCrae's wrist. Zach snapped on the other, then hauled him to his feet.

"Zach?" Tara urged Suzie to go to Alice, who'd returned with the security guard.

Zach pushed McCrae into a chair. "Watch him until the cops get here. I don't feel—" He staggered sideways.

Tara rushed to his side and eased him into a chair. She dropped to her knees in front of him. "How do you feel?"

He stroked her cheek. "Hey, hey, why the tears? You can't…get rid…of me that…" His words came out garbled. He slumped into her arms.

Whittaker helped her ease Zach to the ground.

"Zach, can you hear me? Stay with me."

"What was in the needle?" Whittaker demanded of McCrae.

The guard jostled McCrae, but he refused to answer.

"Make him talk. I need to know what was in that needle," Whittaker ordered. To Alice he said, "Get us some help in here."

Tara positioned Zach so his airway was clear, then counted his respirations. They were shallow and his heart rate too slow, considering the fight he'd just been through. She fought off a paralyzing surge of terror at the thought of him dying.

The guard slapped McCrae's face. "What was in the needle?"

"Check his pockets," Tara yelled.

Beth rushed in with a crash cart. "What do we have?"

"Ten-gauge hypodermic needle with unknown substance to the chest. Breathing suppressed, six breaths per minute. Pulse slow and thready."

"Hook up a saline IV," Whittaker barked. "We'll dilute whatever was in that needle by pushing fluids."

McCrae's gaze lit on Tara and fury seethed in his eyes. "This is all your fault."

Beth gasped at the handcuffed doctor.

The guard tightened his grip on McCrae's shirt collar and gave him a hard shake. "You stabbed that man in front of four witnesses. If you don't want to go down for his murder, I suggest you tell the lady what she wants to hear."

"Insulin. It's insulin."

"Stop," Tara screamed at Beth and grabbed a bag from the cart. "Switch the bag to glucose. Saline will drive his blood sugar even lower. We would have fried his brain within the hour!" Tara hooked the IV line to a bag of glucose and opened the drip full out. "C'mon, Zach. Can you hear me? Don't you give up on me."

"I had to do it," McCrae muttered. "He threatened to expose me." He rocked in the chair, his eyes unfocused. Blood was caked under his nose and splattered across his lab coat. "I was serving the greater good."

Tara let out a disgusted snort.

Riled, McCrae sprang to his feet. But the guard yanked him back. "My treatments were helping people. Curing cancer."

"You're telling me you were peddling some cancer cure? Right here in the hospital?" the guard asked.

"Not peddling. It wasn't about the money. It was never about the money."

"Yeah, sure. Save it for the judge."

Not wanting to deal with McCrae's other atrocities on top of the one ripping her heart out in front of her, Tara pulled a gurney to Zach's prone body, locked its wheels and lowered it to the floor. "Help me get him on this."

Whittaker took Zach's shoulders, and Beth helped Tara with his legs. "On three," Whittaker said. "One, two, *three.*"

Once they'd moved him into a room, Tara checked

his blood pressure again. A hundred over sixty. Still low, but climbing.

Beth hooked the heart-rate monitor to his chest. She squeezed Tara's arm. "Alice has Suzie at the nurse's station. Your friend Kelly is here, too."

"Thank you." Tara brushed the hair from Zach's face. "You can't die on me. Do you hear me? You saved my baby's life. The least you can do is give me a chance to thank you properly."

His blank expression didn't change.

Feeling utterly helpless, she held her hand against his cheek.

Beth pushed a chair up to the bed. "Sit before you fall down."

Suzie tugged Kelly into the room. "I'm sorry, Tara. She was desperate to see you."

"It's okay."

"How is he?" Kelly asked anxiously.

"We don't know yet." Tara lifted Suzie onto her lap and clasped Zach's hand. *Her family.* She couldn't lose them. *Lord, please, don't let him die for saving our lives.*

She bowed her head and let the truth wash over her. Zach had been trying to save her long before today. Saving her from her doubts about God. Saving her from blaming herself for everything that went wrong in her life. But instead of listening to him, she'd grasped at the first indication that he might not share her feelings and rejected him before he could reject her.

I love you, Tara.

Her mind clung to his words. He loved her. And it had sure sounded like he didn't plan to leave her. Not without a fight, anyway. She wanted him in her life. She wanted him to help her raise Suzie, to share their joys and sorrows.

The heart monitor made a funny blip and then another.

Tara set Suzie on the chair and gave her full attention to Zach. She checked the connections. No sign of a problem there. The readout grew more erratic.

"Don't you dare leave me. Do you hear me, Zach? I love you. Suzie loves you. She needs a daddy who'll make sure she eats her veggies. I was just—" Droplets splashed on his bare chest. She swiped at her leaking eyes. "I was scared, Zach. Scared. Please don't leave me."

The beeping grew more erratic.

Beth listened to his respirations. "I'll get Dr. Whittaker."

"Mommy?" Suzie's frightened voice cut through the panic, clouding Tara's thinking.

"It's okay, honey." She hugged her daughter to her chest.

"I'll take her out," Kelly offered.

Suzie giggled and pointed to the bed.

Tara spun around to Zach's smiling eyes looking up at her. "You're awake."

The corners of his eyes crinkled. "You prefer me sleeping?"

"No!"

"Why you sweeping, Dak?" Suzie blurted.

Zach tilted his focus to Suzie for a second or two and then captured Tara's gaze once more. A mischievous light snuck in. "Remember Sleeping Beauty, Suzie?" he asked, never taking his eyes off Tara.

"Yes."

"Well, I was hoping my true love would wake me with her kiss."

Suzie giggled, but Tara choked up, not sure she trusted herself to believe her ears.

"I'll wait outside for Detective Gray." Kelly slipped out of the room.

Zach cupped his hand over Tara's, and she returned her gaze to his. All hint of mischief had disappeared. He looked at her, now, with his heart laid bare.

Waiting.

"You have to close your eyes," Suzie said, drawing a smile from them both.

Zach obeyed and Tara leaned over the bed. Softly, she brushed her lips across his. "I love you," she whispered.

"And I you, my love. And I you."

EPILOGUE

Tara slipped into the small chaplain's office adjoining the hospital chapel. "You wanted to see me?" she asked Melanie, trying not to show her concern.

The young woman looked beautiful in her simple ivory gown, but tears clouded her eyes. "How can I ever thank you for convincing the police to drop the charges against me?"

Tara gave her friend a warm hug. "By living happily ever after."

"You do believe me, don't you? I had no idea McCrae killed that man."

"Of course you didn't. Why would you? Officially, Mr. Parker's death hadn't been ruled suspicious."

"I still can't believe he tried to kill you, too."

"He claims he only hired the guy to scare me. Almost didn't admit to that until they found proof that he paid the shooter in pain prescriptions."

"And he almost succeeded in killing Zach. Was that how he killed Mr. Parker? By stabbing him with insulin?"

"Yes, that's what the police believe, but McCrae's not admitting to it. The coroner says it's next to impossible to prove. From what I've gathered, Deb Parker had a severe reaction to the fever brought on by the treatment, and her husband blamed McCrae, accusing him of pawning off some snake oil on them." Tara dabbed Melanie's cheeks with a tissue. "But don't fret about any of that now. This is your wedding day."

"I'm sorry. I just wanted you to know how grateful I am for all you've done." Melanie caught Tara's hand. "Dr. Whittaker has started me on a new treatment that he's very optimistic will put the cancer into remission."

"That's wonderful!"

The music started, and Melanie's sister slipped into the room. "That's our cue, sis."

"Give me a second to get back to my seat." Tara gave Melanie a warm hug and rushed out the hall exit and around to the back of the chapel. She scooted into the row beside Zach.

Suzie crawled into her lap. "Is the bride dressed like Cinderella, Mommy?"

Tara laughed, not surprised by her daughter's question. Roses adorned every available ledge, and their fragrance infused the room with a fairytale wonder. "She's not dressed quite that fancy, honey," Tara whispered. "But she's just as happy."

The pews were packed with friends and family, nurses and cancer patients. Even Dr. Whittaker had joined them. She'd learned that he'd been under intense pressure from the hospital administrator because of issues with his AP-2000 trials, and that the administrator, not Tara, was the person Whittaker had been complaining about to Alice the day Tara had overheard them talking.

She was still ashamed of herself for thinking he'd murder patients to score estate donations, and was relieved that Miller's Bay Memorial wouldn't be losing their favorite doctor.

The groom stepped onto the small rise at the front of the chapel, his face beaming.

As the gathering rose to honor Melanie's entrance, Zach whispered in Tara's ear, "How long do I have to wait before I can see you in a dress like that?"

Holding Suzie against her galloping heart, Tara leaned her head back against Zach's chest. "Is that a proposal?"

He winked. "Oh, no. I can do better than that."

A warm excitement swirled through Tara's chest at the thought of what she had to look forward to. After nearly losing each other—permanently—her fears of Zach hurting her paled in comparison to the joy she would miss out on by not cherishing each day the Lord gave them to be together.

"Do you forgive me for doubting for a second that my feelings for you were real?" His voice ached with apology. In the two months since McCrae's attack, Zach had showed her in a hundred different ways how much he cared for her and Suzie.

"Trust me," she said with a teasing smile, "I'm enjoying letting you prove just how genuine your feelings are."

He pressed his lips to the top of her head. "Every day for the rest of my life."

* * * * *

Dear Reader,

I have longed to tell Zach's story since first introducing him in *Deep Cover*. I love his character, his devotion to the wife he lost, his honesty about struggling to trust in God's goodness through his loss, and his journey to healing. The story is a tribute to all those who have walked alongside their spouse through the valley of the shadow of death, with a prayer that they embrace the joy of truly living once again.

I lost my mom to cancer many years ago, and my dear friend to the same disease during the writing of this story—a loss that made finishing an emotional roller coaster. My friend had tried numerous experimental treatments over the course of her twenty-year battle, and it was that very real drive to find a cure that prompted the creation of *Critical Condition*'s villain. Of course, although Coley's Toxin, still used in some countries, is an historical treatment for the disease, my villain's use of the drug is purely fictional.

My sincere hope is that, in some small way, Zach and Tara's story inspires you to cherish the gifts of each day and open your heart to new possibilities in the future. At first both Zach and Tara refused to dream of or accept the possibility of a second chance at love, as they held on to past hurts. But God is greater than our past. When one door closes, be ready to trust God to lead you through the new doors He opens.

I love to hear from readers. You can reach me

via email at SandraOrchard@ymail.com, on Facebook at http://www.facebook.com/SandraOrchard, or by snail mail, c/o Harlequin Love Inspired Suspense, 233 Broadway, Suite 1001, New York, NY 10279. To learn about upcoming books and read interesting book extras, please visit me online at www.SandraOrchard.com and sign up for my newsletter for exclusive subscriber giveaways.

Wishing you abundant blessings,
Sandra Orchard

Questions for Discussion

1. Zach admits that at times only sheer determination kept him from blaming God for his wife and child's death. Have you ever blamed God for bad things that happened in your life? With the passage of time, have you been able to see some good come from the experience?

2. Rejected and abandoned by the man who pledged to love her until death do they part, Tara has difficulty believing any man would stick around, partly because she couldn't trust his word, and partly because she shoulders the blame for his leaving. Have you ever had an unbalanced perspective of your role in a problem? How might you have handled it differently?

3. At the start of the book, Tara prioritizes what she perceives to be in her daughter's best interests (i.e. protecting Suzie from what might become a revolving door of father figures) over her own potential happiness. Do you agree with her decision? Why or why not?

4. As a law-enforcement officer, Zach has visited hospitals plenty of times since his wife's death without being affected, but seeing the cancer patients triggers an overwhelming emotional re-

sponse. Are there places or songs or smells or sights that trigger an emotional response in you? How do you handle it?

5. At one point Zach tells Tara that he got pretty tired of hearing people's platitudes after his wife's death. If you've experienced loss, what actions or words on the part of your friends and family did you find helped you the most? What would you urge friends of someone who has lost a loved one *not* to do or say?

6. In addition to the disappointments in her own life, Tara finds it difficult to believe in God, because as a nurse, while she admits to having seen some miraculous recoveries, she's also seen a lot of patients whose prayers go unanswered. Zach says that, just as a parent knows better than to always give a child what she asks for, sometimes God's answer is no. How do you feel or respond when God doesn't seem to be answering your prayers?

7. While Zach experiences an instant attraction to Tara, he chalks it up to her resemblance to his wife, and her little girl. He tells himself that he could never love another woman the way he loved his wife. Do you believe we each have only one true soul mate? Why or why not?

8. Tara admits to herself that as much as she didn't want to depend on a guy ever again, having someone look out for her for a change felt kind of nice. Do you like being in charge of your own destiny? Or do you long to be taken care of? Or vice versa if your situation is the opposite. Why or why not?

9. Although Tara taught Suzie about God and heaven, as much as Tara wanted to, she didn't quite share her daughter's childlike faith. Do you believe in heaven?

10. If, like Tara, you knew you had the power to help justice come sooner, but it meant possible danger to your family, how would you handle the struggle between your maternal calling to protect your child and the need to ensure more innocent lives aren't lost?

11. Tara is a worrywart when it comes to Suzie's health. Are you a worrier? Do you think worrying is a bad thing? Why or why not?

12. Tara's sister is a wonderful encourager and knows her well enough to know when she's hedging. More than that, their relationship is secure enough that Susan feels comfortable challenging Tara about her relationship with Zach. Have you ever challenged, or been challenged by, a close friend or sister? Are you glad you, or she, had the cour-

age to speak her mind? Do you have a friend or family member who could use such a challenge?

13. After their confrontation with Tara's ex-husband, Zach says to her, "Earl has remarried. You can't undo that. You can only move forward from here. Don't let regret over the past steal your *now*." Do you have a regret in your past that is stealing your joy in the present? What could you do to change that?

14. Each critically ill patient feels differently about what lengths they're willing to go to in treating their disease. To what lengths would you be willing to go? Why or why not?

15. By the end of the novel, Tara realizes that her what-if imaginings of all the ways Zach *might* hurt her pale in comparison to the joy she would miss out on by not cherishing each day the Lord gives them to be together. Have you ever let what-ifs keep you from doing something you longed to do, whether pursuing a certain job or relationship, or moving to a different part of the country, or taking a trip? How might your life look different if you'd done that thing?

LARGER-PRINT BOOKS!

**GET 2 FREE
LARGER-PRINT NOVELS
PLUS 2 FREE
MYSTERY GIFTS**

Love Inspired®

SUSPENSE
RIVETING INSPIRATIONAL ROMANCE

Larger-print novels are now available...

YES! Please send me 2 FREE LARGER-PRINT Love Inspired® Suspense novels and my 2 FREE mystery gifts (gifts are worth about $10). After receiving them, if I don't wish to receive any more books, I can return the shipping statement marked "cancel". If I don't cancel, I will receive 4 brand-new novels every month and be billed just $4.99 per book in the U.S. or $5.49 per book in Canada. That's a saving of at least 23% off the cover price. It's quite a bargain! Shipping and handling is just 50¢ per book in the U.S. and 75¢ per book in Canada.* I understand that accepting the 2 free books and gifts places me under no obligation to buy anything. I can always return a shipment and cancel at any time. Even if I never buy another book, the two free books and gifts are mine to keep forever.

110/310 IDN FEH3

Name	(PLEASE PRINT)
Address	Apt. #
City	State/Prov. Zip/Postal Code

Signature (if under 18, a parent or guardian must sign)

Mail to the **Reader Service**:
IN U.S.A.: P.O. Box 1867, Buffalo, NY 14240-1867
IN CANADA: P.O. Box 609, Fort Erie, Ontario L2A 5X3

Not valid for current subscribers to Love Inspired Suspense larger-print books.

**Are you a current subscriber to Love Inspired Suspense books
and want to receive the larger-print edition?
Call 1-800-873-8635 or visit www.ReaderService.com.**

* Terms and prices subject to change without notice. Prices do not include applicable taxes. Sales tax applicable in N.Y. Canadian residents will be charged applicable taxes. Offer not valid in Quebec. This offer is limited to one order per household. All orders subject to credit approval. Credit or debit balances in a customer's account(s) may be offset by any other outstanding balance owed by or to the customer. Please allow 4 to 6 weeks for delivery. Offer available while quantities last.

Your Privacy—The Reader Service is committed to protecting your privacy. Our Privacy Policy is available online at www.ReaderService.com or upon request from the Reader Service.

We make a portion of our mailing list available to reputable third parties that offer products we believe may interest you. If you prefer that we not exchange your name with third parties, or if you wish to clarify or modify your communication preferences, please visit us at www.ReaderService.com/consumerchoice or write to us at Reader Service Preference Service, P.O. Box 9062, Buffalo, NY 14269. Include your complete name and address.

LARGER-PRINT BOOKS!

**GET 2 FREE
LARGER-PRINT NOVELS
PLUS 2 FREE
MYSTERY GIFTS**

Love Inspired

Larger-print novels are now available...

YES! Please send me 2 FREE LARGER-PRINT Love Inspired® novels and my 2 FREE mystery gifts (gifts are worth about $10). After receiving them, if I don't wish to receive any more books, I can return the shipping statement marked "cancel". If I don't cancel, I will receive 6 brand-new novels every month and be billed just $4.99 per book in the U.S. or $5.49 per book in Canada. That's a saving of at least 23% off the cover price. It's quite a bargain! Shipping and handling is just 50¢ per book in the U.S. and 75¢ per book in Canada.* I understand that accepting the 2 free books and gifts places me under no obligation to buy anything. I can always return a shipment and cancel at any time. Even if I never buy another book, the two free books and gifts are mine to keep forever.

122/322 IDN FEG3

Name	(PLEASE PRINT)	
Address		Apt. #
City	State/Prov.	Zip/Postal Code

Signature (if under 18, a parent or guardian must sign)

Mail to the **Reader Service:**
IN U.S.A.: P.O. Box 1867, Buffalo, NY 14240-1867
IN CANADA: P.O. Box 609, Fort Erie, Ontario L2A 5X3

Not valid to current subscribers to Love Inspired Larger-Print books.

**Are you a current subscriber to Love Inspired books
and want to receive the larger-print edition?
Call 1-800-873-8635 or visit www.ReaderService.com.**

* Terms and prices subject to change without notice. Prices do not include applicable taxes. Sales tax applicable in N.Y. Canadian residents will be charged applicable taxes. Offer not valid in Quebec. This offer is limited to one order per household. All orders subject to credit approval. Credit or debit balances in a customer's account(s) may be offset by any other outstanding balance owed by or to the customer. Please allow 4 to 6 weeks for delivery. Offer available while quantities last.

Your Privacy—The Reader Service is committed to protecting your privacy. Our Privacy Policy is available online at www.ReaderService.com or upon request from the Reader Service.

We make a portion of our mailing list available to reputable third parties that offer products we believe may interest you. If you prefer that we not exchange your name with third parties, or if you wish to clarify or modify your communication preferences, please visit us at www.ReaderService.com/consumerschoice or write to us at Reader Service Preference Service, P.O. Box 9062, Buffalo, NY 14269. Include your complete name and address.

LILP11B